The
Remarkable
Everyday

The Remarkable Everyday

'To see the world in a grain of sand...
And eternity in an hour.'
William Blake

A collection of short stories

Legend Press Ltd
13a Northwold Road, London, N16 7HL
www.legendpress.co.uk

Contents © Legend Press 2005

British Library Catologuing in Publication Data available.

ISBN 0-9551032-0-7

Set in times
Printed by Gutenberg Press, Malta

Contents

Legend Press has plans for rapid expansion as a publisher of original, dynamic and high-quality works. It will be maintaining a strong interest in short fiction with a further publication over the next year and will also have a number of further short story initiatives for talented and aspiring writers. In addition, it will be publishing a number of full-length novels over the next 12 months. For more information on Legend Press and its plans for the future, visit www.legendpress.co.uk or email info@legendpress.co.uk

Foreword

If I ever had any doubts about the potential for the short story to rise again to prominence and to battle the novel for prime position on reader's bookshelves, these were dispelled during the composition of this publication. Since announcing its intention to make a mark with the short story and revealing the concept behind the collection, Legend Press has been deluged with interest, support and, most importantly, stories. To give an idea of how the publication was devised, there are two particular moments that stick in my memory.

Firstly, and this only came to prominence later, I was walking the familiar twenty yards to my local shop, absorbed in everyday thought, and I suddenly took a moment to look around. I was surrounded by people bustling along – parents with children, young and old couples, shoppers, kids on bikes, friends talking animatedly, a lone man walking his dog, and even a little old lady dragging a wardrobe.

The reality of the situation really struck home. Here I was, immersed in my own life, and everywhere I looked there were other lives going on at exactly the same time. Each one would be as complex and individual as my own, complete with their unique thoughts, hopes and worries. I remember thinking how fascinating it would be to have a little snapshot of each of their lives and minds.

The second moment occurred when I was travelling home one night – journeys seemingly a hotbed for inspiration. I was considering an appropriate project for Legend Press, a publisher with huge ambitions across the literary range. I wanted the publication to be something original, something with scope and something that really laid down a marker for the company as an innovative and successful publisher.

It was then that I saw the perfect vehicle – the short story.

Overlooked for far too long, the short story can encapsulate everything literature has to offer into a concentrated nutshell. Not only that, but when placed side-by-side, as a collective force, the stories can offer a unique diversity and range simply not possible in the standard novel, for all the latter's great merits. Particularly in a society that is less inclined to wait and one that is in love with the quick and snappy, the short story seems designed to fit.

Then, in an instant, I saw that here was the chance to offer that snapshot of life within a single book. Having already staggered at just how much is going on at any given moment, with each day's immeasurable potential as a basis for story-telling, the title appeared naturally: *'The Remarkable Everyday'*. One character, one day and infinite scope for writer imagination and creativity.

It seems that writers from far and wide shared Legend Press' enthusiasm and passion for this idea. Submissions were received not only from throughout the UK but from the United States, Canada, Spain, New Zealand, Australia and South Africa.

We also benefited from an immense level of support from sources including art councils; literacy trusts; publishing and literary magazines; writing groups; and even organisations running literacy and writing courses. In addition, we set up a short story competition, though international writing website FanStory.com, offering cash prizes for the winners. In fact, the entries were of such a high standard that the top two have been included in the collection.

Then it came down to the difficult decision of selecting the best and most appropriate stories. As I previously mentioned, one of the fantastic benefits of the short story collection is that it can offer so much diversity without losing any of the narrative concentration. Therefore, one of the basic aims was to create a publication that every reader would be able to take something from.

Of course, one of main benefits of the short story collection written by different authors is the huge variety in tone, style and delivery. While a number of the stories are very hard-hitting in theme and content, this is obviously carried out in very different ways by each of the writers. Therefore, very much as a part of the depiction, a couple of stories do contain strong language and content. The others would be appropriate for readers of any age.

To further complement the collection, an introduction has been written by the leading short story scholar, Nena Skrbic. Her insightful and highly-regarded work has focused, in particular, on Virginia Woolf, one of the great short fiction writers and a major influence behind *'The Remarkable Everyday'*. Nena offers her interpretation of the stories as an exploration of contemporary life and society and considers how this raw depiction of modern reality strikes a chord with the reader though partial-identification. She further emphasises the short story as the perfect medium for focusing on the individual, in which 'the potency of the lived moment replaces history'.

So this mammoth project is finally complete, and I would like to personally thank the many writers who have submitted work for consideration. With a public rapidly turning again to the short story, it is reassuring to know that there is such a wealth of writing talent ready and waiting to satisfy this appetite. Most importantly of all, next time I am outside my local shop, I can look around and know that a little of the vibrancy of everyday life has been captured.

Tom Chalmers
Publishing Director, Legend Press

Nena Skrbic completed her Ph.D. on the short fiction of Virginia Woolf at the University of Hull, UK. She is the author of 'Wild Outbursts of Freedom: Reading the Short Fiction of Virginia Woolf' *(Greenwood Press: 2004). Other work includes* 'A Foreign Country: Crossing Cultural Boundaries in the Short Fiction' *in* 'Trespassing Boundaries: Virginia Woolf's Short Fiction' *Eds. Kathryn N. Benzel and Ruth Hoberman (Palgrave Macmillan: 2004). Currently she is a tutor of English language and literature at Thomas Danby College of Further Education, Leeds, UK.*

Introduction

*'With intermittent shocks, sudden as the springs of a
tiger, life emerges heaving its dark crest from the sea.
It is to this we are bound, as bodies to wild horses.
And yet we have invented devices for filling up the
crevices and disguising these fissures.'*
(Virginia Woolf, *The Waves*)

These eight stories about love, longing and infidelity; self-deception, self-doubt and self-loathing cover the sum of human unhappiness – the pretensions and neuroses, the confessions and concealments, the resentments and antagonisms at the heart of our everyday lives – while also exploring how we can draw consolation and spirit even when plagued with fear and doubt.

Highly influenced by the early twenty-first century context in which they are realised, yet illustrating the unchangeability of human nature, they demonstrate that there are plenty of discoveries to be made within the fissures and absences of day-to-day living – family secrets, adulterous relationships, the fear of growing old unhappy or in the wrong body. In each story, the zones of comfortable certainty – the ways in which we can delude ourselves that we exist happily (marriage, family, work, and even gender) – have become alien. In all, Prozac, cocaine, alcohol and sex offer alternative means of self-preservation and world-forgetfulness. Psychologically analogous, each of these stories home in on chronically tired and oppressively self-aware subjects (or anxious spirits) whose self-communion is punctuated by a series of vexing personal questions. All this happens in such a compressed way that it makes the claustrophobia within them all the more compelling.

Justin Elliott's *'Tuesday'* is a mock-playful – yet deadly serious – insight into the post-op life of a thirty-three-year-old male sex-change patient (a new sociological type), who – with a measure of ennui and exhaustion – is about to embark upon the '[first] chapter of her romantic life'. Clichéd, pantomimic representations of femininity are the paradigm here as 'tottering on cruel heels' the modern day heroine begins her emotional journey: 'It was stupid, but she needed to feel the full range of what it meant to be a woman, even if that meant exposing herself to danger. She needed the full, unequivocal experience'. Clearly exposing the underlying insecurities of life lived 'from the other side of the genital divide', Elliott examines the partly consoling, partly threatening realm of female identity. His language is visceral and bold and his stark style of description desentimentalises the soft-focus allure of his heroine's romantic expectations with sharpness and clarity. Journeying back and forth between images of novelettish romance and the erotically-charged, Elliott gives us an unconventional entry into female consciousness:

'It had all been worth it. All the drugs, the vomiting, the pain, the self-disgust. Cutting her rectum with a knife so the blood would drip into the toilet bowl like a period. Staring at herself for hours in the mirror, crying at her gratuitous muscularity, and hideous, distended Adam's apple. All these had been steps on the parabolic curve of self-discovery.'

The backdrop of *'Tuesday'* is far from reassuring and there is a feeling of overwhelming, almost frightening immensity. The protagonist's perception of the world is relayed almost entirely through an economical language of images, which in a very modernist way, establish a psychological viewpoint rather than a narrative. These images have an exaggerated, stranger-than-fiction reality – the alienated and anonymous figure of the kite flyer and the dying seal, for example, communicate the strength of the protagonist's emotion directly:

'She offered her hand, but he ignored it. They walked in silence, up the steps from the spit, up into the tufty grass on the top of the cliff, past the ice-cream van with its sad-looking one-armed attendant, past the balloon seller, who looked sadder still. The balloons were shrunken in the chill breeze, saggy and contracted like an old woman's breasts.'

Abandoned, tragic and down-at-heel, these ghostly images of isolation are the visual correlatives of an enigmatic mental landscape. It is on this visual storytelling, which forces the reader to rely on their visual sense rather than the words on the page, that the eloquence of the story finally depends.

'Wednesday' by E.C. Seaman is the tragedy of a woman who has died without ever having lived. An exploration of the vulnerable, submissive side to the female psyche, this story exposes the tragedy of women's impotence from the narrative viewpoint of a wife whose want of intimacy with her husband and desire 'to end the charade' of her married life has ended in suicide. With no 'human' content as such, this reflective tale of wifely unhingement – narrated by her ghost to her husband – exposes the dangerous psychological implications of leaving things unsaid and communicates the despair of mental depression, in all its pathological grief and lucidity: 'I've always hoped to make that one bold gesture that will eventually crack your reserve, make you fling your arms around me and say you love me; that will finally force you to feel'. The uncanny is a handy metaphor for the ghostly vacancy that exists between the two seemingly incompatible and unconnected worlds on either side of the Mars/Venus divide:

'…you and I speak the same language and after all these years, we still can't understand one another. Maybe your brain's wired differently to mine, or you learnt a different form of speech. Perhaps when I say 'love', you hear 'hate'. Or do you hear something even less relevant, a random word like 'lawnmower' or 'fruit'?'

A raw exploration of feminine insecurity and suppressed individuality, *'Wednesday'* communicates the intolerance and fear of difference that colours other stories in the collection, such as *'Tuesday'*: 'You want the free-spirited river nymph, but without all the darkness that drives my obsession. But extract that passion and what will be left of me?' This exploration of the estrangement, indifference and disengagement that can be at the heart of human relationships raises the possibility of never truly knowing another, even in marriage.

Silence and incommunicability become central themes in Brett Pransky's *'Friday'* – the story of an unhappily married university lecturer about to experience an unanticipated *éclaircissement*. The beginning of the story documents the mood switch from the dream-world to the tedium and predictability of the protagonist's married life. Strong on quotidian atmosphere, the story documents a lost state of perfection – the broken door handle, the rusted mailbox and the four-year-old sedan carry the burden of history and are pertinent in amplifying the story's complementary themes of memory and mortality, entrapment and freedom. For the story's ageing protagonist, sex is a way of turning back the clock, giving the illusion of mutability and transformation:

'He noticed a small coffee stain on the back of her robe, and couldn't help but form a nostalgic smile. In that moment, for just an instant, the poorly built, poorly furnished box apartment became a different place, a better place, and he became a different person, a younger person.'

Immersed in questions about the nature of human longing

and escapism and drawing on the instabilities of 'unfulfilled desire and undesired guilt', *'Friday'* probes the undersurface of common everyday experiences. Pransky does present his protagonist in a sensitive and honest way, however, and part of the issue for the reader is that they can't help feeling guilty that they empathise with him. The end of the tale – though hopeful – gives a realistic sense of moral discomfort.

A sense of discovery and journeying (inner and outer) is implicit in the metaphor of the train journey in *'Monday'* by Sarah James. James does not privilege any one voice, but divides the story into three separate sections that give an insight into the psychogeography of her characters – Catherine, a lonely woman seeking 'a different, more exciting world'; Ben, a mobile phone salesman dealing with paranoia triggered by his struggle to balance work and family; and Phil, an ageing, lonely conductor, undergoing hypnotherapy to boost his self-confidence. With varying degrees of self-absorption and desperation, the characters contemplate the monotony of their lives and the routes they could have taken. This is quite literally storymaking on the move.

The question of how we communicate with and interpret others is important here. The gaps between the sections avoid each voice segueing into the next and demonstrate the characters' absent relation to each other. It is the disjuncture between public and private identity that is fascinating in this story. The characters do not speak at all. Rather, they project subjective interpretations onto each other. In the case of Catherine and Ben, a whole relationship (complete with accusations, misunderstandings and jealousies) is played out paralinguistically, which precludes the necessity of interacting at all. The end of the story superbly illustrates this premise.

Lea Hurst's *'Thursday'* is the story of a recently widowed woman whose instinct for survival seems to have taken a different form since the death of her husband. An abstracted storyline follows her trip to a supermarket where her subsequent visual encounter with a bunch of peaches triggers thoughts, memories and associations connected to her married life:

'She could see again the sun slanting through the old lace curtains and hear the squeaky foreign traffic noises floating up from the square. They had called each other silly fools and slurped at the yellow flesh of the peaches'.

Hurst's metaphorical use of the peaches epitomises the conceptual focus of the modern short story and its reliance on the suddenly seized, symbolically-charged detail. This sort of shorthand – which Allan Pasco describes as the short story's affinity for 'the essential truth or idea or image which rises above time and negates whatever chronological progression the work possesses' – despite its simplicity makes the short story far more effective aesthetically. The abiding impression in this story is not of time passing but of a series of visual images that resist continuity and 'connectedness' and testify to the precarious qualities of life itself. We know better, the story seems to say, than to look for any sense of coherence.

Miguel Ylareina's *'Saturday'* continues the themes and motifs of the other stories in the collection, including the sense of the familiar infused with unease. A young black girl awakes and looks out of her bedroom window, only to find a picture of a noose painted on the door of her white neighbour's shed. Set in the present day, it is an odd historical jolt. The parallel montage of violence and the beauty of the natural world (the fruit harvest signifies nature and its cycles in harmony with human life) implies a reassuring order that is about to be unsettled. This point is vividly made in the story's opening metaphor that describes the element of treacherous uncertainty, which characterises life in a precarious world:

'Sometimes life changes slowly, like the tide wearing away a cliff. Sometimes life changes all at once, like a big section of cliff tumbling into the ocean, revealing something deeper within, something new.'

Felissa's emotional journey to make sense of the tragedy, to analyse exactly what happened to her grandfather and to consider who was to blame for his death broaches interesting philosophical questions about history and racial identity. On the one hand, her determination to learn the truth sympathises with our eagerness to perceive a dramatic pattern and significance in experience; on the other, her confusion over the exact status of the story critiques our self-satisfied way of looking at the world by interrogating the presumptions and easy conclusions we make about the past. This is because how these presumptions and conclusions are arrived at may be influenced by stereotyped attitudes and paranoid belief engendered by upbringing, society and ideological beliefs. The story's tension lies in the contrarious ways in which Felissa and her friend attempt to interpret and shape their discovery. Lorman is deemed incapable of conceptualising Felissa's fear: 'How could he ever really understand what it meant to be black? She could see he didn't share her fright, her sick feeling, wondering what they'd find'. Her neighbour's dream of memorialising the shed to 'show what pathetic prejudice, misused power, and the miscarriage of justice does to people' is an introduction to our contemporary political scene and is an equally relevant metaphor at the beginning of the twenty-first century in relation to the current battle against terrorism.

'Thursday' by Joel Willans is full of the quality of real life and looks cynically at commercialised modernity and the ties that bind us to the 'rat race'. The central character, a successful, but disillusioned media salesman, cuts a lonely Kafka-esque figure. With his integrity virtually undone by

the trappings of his 'comfortable lifestyle', he faces a difficult choice between morality and the path of least resistance: 'I like working in Soho and I like the cash I get, but is that really enough? I certainly don't want to be doing this forever. The problem is, there's nothing for me to do instead'. In the manner of a morality play, Duncan Parks' dilemma reflects a search for moral order in a world that seems in its senility. The images of a cruel and indifferent nature imply a no longer reassuring, immutable reality that can be relied upon:

> 'The sky is the colour of a battleship. It feels as if the sun
> can't be bothered. People march with their heads down
> past the terraced growth of houses that cramp the street.
> Cars squat in the road, spewing fumes and beeping like
> angry robots.'

Attempts to express an identity apart from the collective are angry and territorial. The social space is hostile, the trip to work a Darwinian fight for survival. *'Thursday'* represents a sick culture with its life and colour drained away: 'I rush down the steps into the underground. It smells of piss and old beer. The harsh light bleaches faces, making everyone look ill. I glide down the escalator, past adverts for West End shows, makeup and mobile phones'. The adverts offer an ironic comment on consumerism and human happiness and underline the extent to which social identity is essentially fake – the surface-self a construct of others. As if to compensate, we create a synthetic, fake reality that is meant to offer us some naive hope. The images of 'harsh neon light' in Blue Peter-style offices allow a surrealist retreat and cocaine addiction provides a spurious means of attaining self-awareness.

'Thursday' demonstrates the unfashionableness of moral guilt in the early twenty-first century. Parable-like, the story's events are symbolic, with the incidents in it working

as illustrations of the moral point. The characters, apart from the protagonist, offer a dichotomous view, symbolising a selfishness at the heart of society and the self-regarding, image-related basis of human interaction. In the manner of a moral story, *'Thursday'* is closed-ended, explanatory, satisfying. Duncan Parks emerges with his integrity intact, his faith in the world restored.

'Sunday' by Sophie Mackintosh is a heavily introspective story that describes a monumental day in the life of a mother after the death of her child. Monumental because over and above its tragedy, it asserts the value of living. Take, for instance, the sensuous opening paragraph, which describes the rush of happiness and the desire to epiphanise it:

'For a moment when I wake up, I see the sun streaming through my window and I feel a flash of happiness. I feel its warmth on my skin and luxuriate in its feeling, for one golden second. And then I remember what day it is, and immediately the golden second is tarnished.'

Begetting a narrative that is ambiently reminiscent of Virginia Woolf's concept of 'the moment', the story resists chronology. Instead, a series of elliptically connected images reference the life of the narrator's daughter – a swing in the park, for instance, is burdened with association and establishes connections to a lost historical context, giving the story large-scale coherence. Moreover, recurring images and memories of her daughter's care-free childhood stand proxy for the tragedy of her own lost youth, of remembered sensations, impressions, experiences, of sad memories and ideals. It is at this paralysing juncture between passive nostalgia and the present moment – which carries on regardless of the narrator's non-engagement – that the story operates.

'Sunday' highlights the psychological function that stories serve – how people tell (or re-tell) stories to make sense of

their lives and the way we console ourselves by repetition. We get the sense that the narrator has re-visited her child's death countless times – working and re-working the story of the accident over and over. At the end, against all the evident odds, she attains a small triumph against chance and fate: 'As I start to drift off, I think to myself: today I have started to live again. It may only be small things that I have done, but now that I have done them I feel so much better'. In *'Sunday'* it is the very 'dailyness' of our lives that – ironically – gives us direction and assures us of a stable pattern behind the violent and confused state of things.

It is in the intensely human and exceptionally honest reflection of life and human vulnerabilities that the contemporaneity and, indeed, endurance of this whole collection lies. In working out the story of the moment, the writers have produced a compellingly readable insight into contemporary urban experience. The choice of the short story as a medium emphasises the collection's tight focus on the individual. It is this inwardness and way of looking at the short story in terms of the epic-scale versus the human-sized that underlines a particularly modernist use of the short fiction form, one in which the potency of the lived moment replaces history. As Margaret Atwood observes: 'The fictional writer who writes to no one is rare' and it is safe to say that with their rawness and emotional content, these writers have captured the common reader. These are characters who we may – no, will – end up half-identifying with.

Reference

Atwood, Margaret. *'Negotiating with the Dead: A Writer on Writing'* (pp.127) (CUP, 2002).

Pasco, Allan H. *'On Defining Short Stories'* (pp126). In *'New Short Story Theories'* Ed. Charles E. May (Ohio University Press, 1994), (pp.114-30).

Tuesday

By
Justin Elliott

The Remarkable Everyday

Mary O'Connor huddled before the fire, cursing her new found sensitivity, yet revelling in it at the same time. It was not even October, in a part of the country that was supposed to be sub-tropical, but still she felt the draft like an arctic breeze. It rippled the hem of her skirt, climbing up her legs with all the clumsy determination of an English explorer. She would never have noticed it before, when her body had been harder, stronger. But now, well, she might have to think about putting the central heating on. One fire was never enough.

Fraggle, the geriatric ginger tom, glanced up at her myopically. He was leaning against the chimney breast, grunting as he attempted to stick a cleansing tongue into a distant crevice. He wasn't as flexible as he once was, so this was easier said than done. His eyes were shot, too, and he was deaf in one ear, so that he always turned to his right to face danger, when danger invariably came from the left. He was largely helpless, a thing which ate, slept, and bumped into coffee tables.

In his dreams, though, he was still the scourge of all things rodent. He would leap about, sometimes, eyes tight shut, batting away at invisible beasts. Mary identified with his self-deception. She had long since been performing a similar trick upon herself.

She reached behind the curry-stained back of the old armchair, retrieving the precious sketch from its featherbed of dried poppadum shards. She had been fussing over the drawing for a few days now. It served as her cover, her reason to get even closer to her new friend. She twisted it this way and that, wondering if, by some accident, she had in fact any talent.

No, it was rubbish. Mary had a way with words (hoped, in fact, to make a living from them), but she had no skill with the brush at all. The sea was lifeless, the boats unrealistic. She had ideas, but there was something missing between her brain and her fingers. Something was lost in translation. She peered closer, the hunched form in the foreground nevertheless stirring something peculiar within. The woman, the artist Sylvia Carey, seen from the rear as she painted her own masterpiece. Her arms were spread, like some baby albatross facing into the wind for its first flight. A beautiful, delicate creature. With a cracking pair of breasts.

Sylvia Carey. It made her sound like some feminist professor. Or maybe a downtrodden northern housewife. The best names always inspired a sense of mystery. The Christian name was for Sylvia Plath. The surname was her ex-husband's, a lecturer at some undisclosed university. He'd divorced her, incredibly, as if such women were commonplace.

Mary prized these little snippets of information, which in time she hoped would develop into a full biography. Sylvia, she had decided, was very nearly the perfect woman. This made her an ideal case study.

She sighed, then chucked another log onto the fire. It spat as it hit, too green, too wet. Dirty smoke pulsed through the room, adding yet another layer of tar to the peeling, yellow-brown wallpaper. The cottage's previous owner, Uncle Frioc, had smoked fifty woodbines a day for sixty years, claiming that the nicotine stained walls were, in fact, a discontinued variety of Dulux magnolia. Poor old Frioc. He had developed a nasty cough in later years, which his neighbours had attributed to lung cancer. Finally, after months of badgering, he had agreed to visit the doctor, only to get run over on the way to the surgery by a trainee chemist. A post-mortem revealed that his cough had actually stemmed from an allergic reaction to ghee. Despite a lack of credible alternatives, the Star of Jaipur had refused to admit any liability.

The Remarkable Everyday

Mary scratched absently at her crotch, which still retained a vestigial itchiness. To balance this out, she ran a finger between the fulsome protrusion of her breasts, circling each nipple until it started to tingle. She had not yet started to take them for granted, which she supposed would be a sign in itself, when it finally happened. Proper ladies almost always took their chests for granted, or at least claimed to.

Time to go. Time to take a walk. Dr Alleyne had suggested she should keep moving to ensure that her parts were kept properly aired. So she shrugged herself into a nice Laura Ashley number, applying a subtle shade of lippy that complemented the soft pastels of her dress. She was a size fourteen, mostly – which was disappointing – but she took comfort in the fact that women generally were getting bigger. It wasn't a problem, not really. She had long since accepted that she would never be a supermodel. Womanly. That was the best adjective for her.

Outside, the streets were busy with those who had come for the annual music festival and the dregs of the season's holidaymakers. In a few weeks the town would go into its annual hibernation. Mary wondered what she would do then. She liked to sit by the window in her cottage, peering out at the countless passers-by, trying to work out what they were thinking. Eye-up the men, empathise with the women. Or vice-versa, depending on her mood.

She clumped down the steep zigzag of the Digey, tottering on cruel heels. She was a bit unstable, lacking as she did the necessary width of hips. She almost tripped in the gutter, slick with rain, only managing to right herself by grabbing hold of a passing midget. She thought she recognised him. Johnny, was it? Ronny? Something of a local celebrity. A jockey, maybe. Whatever, the pygmy cursed, looking up at her as if she were the freak. A B&B sign clacked about in the breeze, like something from a Western. A cat hissed, arching its back and looking at her with a degree of suspicion that was unusual, even for an animal that hunted rats for a living. A boy sniggered. She ignored him, wobbling out along Fore Street, then doubling back towards the lifeboat station.

She liked the lifeboat men. They looked very smart in their orange oilskins. Very brave. Very, oh, why not say it? Very hunky. She had a dream, sometimes, of being rescued.

"Hey, it's the fuckin' ladyboy!" a voice called out. "Oi, chick with a dick! Is it true you can fuck yourself up your own ass?"

Mary groaned, spinning round on her heels, and saw that Billy London, chief among her tormentors, was pointing at her. Billy it was who had plastered the posters across the town, offering niche-market, weirdo sex. He'd found her mobile number from somewhere and printed it out in bold, underlined, italicised text. Perverts from miles around still called her on a regular basis.

She prayed that, for once, he might find something else to keep him amused. He had been following her around for weeks now, on his own or in a group of his friends. The kid was evil, plain and simple.

She hurried along the harbour side, dropping down onto the sand in a billow of frock and manic, windmilling arms. Bad move. Her heels dug into the sand, sending her headfirst into a knickers-up sprawl.

She got to her feet, spitting out oily sand and seaweed. There were two of them this time. Billy and his queen bitch, spotty girlfriend Kaz.

"Please leave me alone," Mary pleaded. "I've not done anything to you."

"Not true," Billy disagreed. "Ladyboy."

"I'm not a ladyboy. How many times do I have to tell you?"

"It's disgustin'," girlfriend opined.

Kaz glared at Mary, her knees flexing in an involuntary curtsey as if she were seeking to demonstrate her lack of encumberment down below. God, she was ugly. Her face was swollen, bruised here and there, the colour of a cow's nose. Her cheeks resembled a couple of full udders, a mass of spotty teats leaking their own milky puss. She was like many teenagers – self-centred and obnoxious, come too early to the full ugliness of adulthood. It made her awkward, and malevolent, almost as bad as her boyfriend.

"Disgustin'," Billy agreed.

"What?" Mary sputtered in exasperation. "What's disgusting? I'm just a normal woman."

Billy took a step closer. He was a head shorter than Mary, who was admittedly quite tall for a woman. But he was far more muscular than she, with a natural bulkiness that was as yet unencumbered by fat. In later life, he would doubtless develop an excessive number of chins and bellies, but for now poor genetics were being outweighed by a runaway metabolism. Fat was converted as fast as it was ingested. Brief, stupendous biological alchemy!

"Normal women," he said, "do not have cocks."

He looked at Kaz, who nodded her head, peering up at him with the kind of adoration normally reserved for dictators. It was hard to see how he might command such devotion, but then Hitler was hardly a looker. Mussolini was a fatty. There were precedents.

"I do not have a penis," Mary said quietly.

Billy shifted his bulk. Such a transportation of dangerous materials would normally have required council approval. "Prove it."

Mary crossed her arms, scowling her displeasure. She knew she was very alone, isolated and vulnerable to Billy's cruelty. His fists were clenched, muscles were squaring off against each other as if jealous of each nerve impulse. Yet this had gone on far too long. She was sick of the little prick. And so what if he hit her? Deep down, in the part of her that experienced a sneaky thrill at the pain of injured boxers, she imagined how she might look with a bloody nose. Like a battered wife, maybe. It was a terrible, beautiful image. Mary snuffled at the potential tragedy, then grew irritated by the accompanying dribble of mucus. There was nothing clever or tragic about snot, it was merely icky. She stamped her foot, feeling further delight at the inconstancy of her mood.

"Why don't you show me yours, first?" she suggested. "We could compare and find out who's the real man."

Billy said nothing, for a moment. His mouth hung open, letting a stream of tobacco-laced dribble settle in his stubble. He stared, unblinking, as if someone had cut out his eyelids.

But only for a moment. There was a globble, and a gloop. His features were suddenly infused with blood, making his head swell to dangerous proportions.

"You're dead, you weird fucker," he hissed.

He made a lunge, his fingers entwining with the lacy flounce of Mary's cleavage. He flung her around in a rough circle, sending her crashing into the wall with a dull thud. Mary groaned, sliding roughly down to land in a dazed, tearful heap. She heard Kaz laughing, the girl's nasal shriek at least two octaves higher than Billy's deep chortle.

Ah, let him look. Let the little bastard look.

But Billy had a knife. It gleamed in the soft Cornish sunshine.

"I'm gonna prove this once and fur all," he said. "And then I'm gonna cut it off."

He spat on the blade, then rubbed it against his thigh. Kaz sniggered. Billy glared at her. Torture was a serious business.

"What are you doin'?"

Mary rolled onto her back. She looked up to see a small, skinny, ginger kid glaring at Billy with dead eyes.

Owen. She felt a curious flare of emotion when she saw him – guilt, sadness and lust. The three were inextricably linked.

They had met the night before, outside the youth centre. He had been looking a bit upset, she had been feeling a bit lonely. He had offered her a bite of his pastie. Afterwards, he had kissed her. There had surely been something in between, but Mary couldn't remember anything other than the pastie and the snog. Teeth had clashed. He had mumbled an apology as if he had done something wrong. But Mary had loved his awkwardness, which had sat so comfortably with her own. If she had been braver, she might have asked to see him again.

"Just teaching the perv a lesson, sos," Billy replied, rather carefully. "You can give us a hand, if you want."

"Let her go," Owen ordered.

Billy scowled. "It's a him, not a her. Do you really think I'd hit a woman?"

"I dunno," Owen murmured. "Does Kaz count?"

"Aw, come on," Billy wheedled. "Let's not fuck around, eh? All we gotta do is put this bitch straight, then we can be on our way. Honour will be satisfied and all that."

"Honour, Bill?"

"Yeah. Gotta make a stand. Let this go and before you know it we'd have kiddy-fuckers and all sorts roamin' round."

"Feederpiles!" Kaz squealed.

"So," Billy pressed, "you in?"

Owen stood still for a moment, head hanging loosely to one side, as if someone had sneaked up behind him and cut all the tendons in one side of his neck.

"Nah," he said finally. "Don't think so."

"Why not?"

"Because you did my mum."

Ah, the ghost town thing again. Crisp packets rolled across the sand, not quite tumbleweed, but close enough. Upturned dinghies, like cow carcasses, bleached by the sun. Even the seagulls were transformed, the adolescents as malevolent, as beaky as any vulture. Billy flinched. He looked guiltily at Kaz, whose face, with the exception of her spots, was suddenly drained of colour. The blackheads and the whiteheads remained, thrown into lurid, pussy relief by the pasty hue of the rest of her features. She shrieked, then started to cry like an Italian.

"But his mum's a whore," Kaz wailed. "An' a cheap un, too! I've heard her only charges a fiver for a wank – that'd barely get you a snog in Penzance! What does that make me? You fuckin' promised me, Billy! You promised me the first time I sucked you off you'd-"

"Look, it meant nothing," Billy interjected. "I was just curious, all right? And actually, I did it for you as well. I thought that maybe her could teach me a few things that I could use on you. I'll show you later, if you'll let me."

"Fuck off," she hissed. And, after a brief, liquid pause, "Why, though? What's her got that I haven't?"

Billy held his hands out wide as if he had been nailed to a cross. Mary was struck by how well he could act the martyr. The kid was an actor all right, with an actor's capacity for bullying, self-indulgence and deceit. He would probably tread the boards, in later life, if the Boards didn't get him first.

"Nothing, babe," he answered. "Her ain't got any tits, for a start, and she's looser than a wizard's sleeve. It was like I'd been fuckin' paralysed. But you, well, you got brilliant tits and everything else an' all. I swear, now that I've tried it, I don't ever wanna do it again." He shivered, and hugged his arms about his chest. "I feel dirty," he concluded.

Mary was aware, even if Billy was not, that Owen had turned a rather pronounced shade of scarlet. She supposed that she should really take advantage of the situation, make her getaway while her tormentor's attention was elsewhere. Yet, for whatever reason, she could not. It was partly down to her fascination with the primal, timeless, immeasurably coarse nature of Kaz's pain. Mary was always on the look out for such conflagrations of female emotion, which she might, with practice, be able to weave into her own life. The majority of her emotions were, more's the pity, vicarious ones.

The hurt. Despair. Guilt. Guilt? That was odd.

Mostly, though, it was that she was touched by Owen's chivalry. She could not think of abandoning him. That he – poor, skinny and clearly wronged – should leap to her defence! In this light, he looked almost unbearably cute. Maybe she would let him have her, later.

Sometimes, Mary's only defence was flippancy.

Somewhere in the mêlée, the black knight had managed to butter up his fair maiden. Kaz was still trying to seem upset, but, deep down, she had probably always known that this was to be her lot in life. It had only been a matter of time before Billy fucked one of his friends' mothers.

"Surely it's better I get it out my system now, eh?" Billy cajoled. "Better now than when we're married?"

The tears stopped in an instant. God, were girls really that easy to manipulate? Mary suddenly felt ashamed of her own probable gullibility. Thrilled by it, too. What if some man should someday treat her in a similar fashion? It was terrible. Made her blood boil. Oh.

"You want to marry me?" Kaz breathed.

"Well, eventually."

Owen snorted, which didn't go down too well. If Billy had been feeling a hint of remorse before, this evaporated in an instant. He lashed out, catching Owen a stunning blow on the point of the chin. Owen slid down the wall, his head lolling to a rest against Mary's shoulder.

"If you weren't my mate, I'd have fuckin' knifed ya," Billy hissed. He then scowled at Mary, who pressed herself hard against the slimy weeds. "And as for you-"

"Leave it, Bill," Kaz said. "Neither of 'em are worth it." She sniffed, and spat in Mary's direction.

Billy drew himself up to his full height, which was roughly knee-high to a baby tyrannosaur. His eyes burned red. Very Spielbergian.

"Later, ladyboy," he hissed.

Seizing Kaz by the hand, he strode out across the sand, casting a murderous glance at the group of seagulls that had settled down to watch proceedings. They followed him about wherever he went, much as their more honest cousins might follow a trawler. He walked though life with serrated toecaps, tearing up the rice paper, leaving carrion in his wake. Scavengers recognised this.

Mary turned her head to one side. Owen was looking at her.

"Thank you," she said. "Are you hurt?"

"A bit. You?"

"No, not really."

Owen took out a cigarette. He lit it between trembling fingers, taking a deep drag that began somewhere in front of his nose and ended near his toes. His whole body laid itself open to the smoke. He offered Mary a puff. She refused.

"Is what you said about him and your mum true, Owen?"

Owen nodded. He looked out across the sand. Billy and

31

Kaz had stopped among the boats for a snog. Explicit body parts requisitioned blood from more reasoned, thinking regions in a series of sniggers and shivers. Kaz had stiff nips. Billy had a hard-on. Both of them got off on the making-up part of a relationship.

"Do you hate anything, ladyboy?" Owen asked distractedly.

"I am not a ladyboy," Mary answered automatically. "Remember?"

"Sorry, Mary."

"But anyway, yes, of course I do. Just because I'm a woman, it doesn't automatically follow that I will love everything."

"Hmmn."

"So, I hate Zoë ffrench-Batistuta, of the Stripy Pony Literary Agency. She has rejected every manuscript I have ever sent her. Oh, and Billy London. And his father, too."

"You know Jack?"

"I do. It was him who told Billy about me. And now the whole town knows. Billy saw to that. Have you seen the posters?"

"Yeah. He did them on his dad's computer. I helped him with the colours."

"Thanks."

"Sorry. He kind of made me. He's colour blind, you see. Red-green. He can't tell the difference between blood and sick." Owen took another drag on his cigarette. Mary saw that his fingers were trembling.

"Does he bully you?"

"He bullies everyone, apart from his old man."

"I see."

"So how did Jack find out, then?" Owen asked. "I mean, I don't think anyone would know by looking at you. You're stacked."

Mary felt herself go red. She could sense that he had hidden depths. She had sensed it the night before, the thrill of confirmation made her belly scrunch up. Beneath the pained, coarse exterior, there was a sweetie waiting to be set free. Hmmnn.

"Thanks," she murmured. "But Jack used to work for the Health Authority. He had access to all sorts of stuff."

"I'll bet."

Owen closed his eyes. Mary tapped a finger against a tooth, as she always did when she was nervous. She steeled herself, looking for a little more in the way of courage, while trying to seem light-hearted and not at all desperate. And she was desperate. For someone to talk to, if nothing else.

"I think that maybe I should repay your kindness, Owen," she said in her most appropriate voice, the one she had used when first meeting with her plastic surgeon. "Maybe we could go for a walk, later? Perhaps I could buy you an ice-cream or something."

Owen's eyes opened, one at a time. He frowned. He looked up at the sky, then down at the sand, as if trying to find his bearings. Finally, he shrugged, and nodded. Mary clapped her hands. She couldn't help it. He really was very cute indeed.

"I'll meet you at the lighthouse at six, then."

"All right," he agreed.

****

But it was not even lunchtime yet, and Mary had a few more things to take care of before embarking on this latest – or, to put it another way, first – chapter of her romantic life. She sat outside in the Sloop Jethro B's beer garden, watching the kids zip about on their skateboards, buzzing the Festival visitors and hardier tourists. There were a few Americans in the throng, doubtless taking a day out to do 'the real England', before moving on to do 'the real France' on Wednesday, Germany on Thursday, and so on. What must they think of it all? The English were becoming a race of dull-witted, ugly, hopelessly rude simpletons.

She took a sip from her drink, a vodka, lime and lemonade. It was a fairly gay drink, but that was okay cause she was a girl, and girls, as she kept reminding herself when the world threatened to grow too complicated, were just gay men with tits and a fanny. People used to take the piss before, but now it was okay. Okay to have a low alcohol tolerance. Okay to have a weak bladder. It was all part of being a woman. With every major advantage, there came a fairly trivial disadvantage. It was okay.

She was shivering. It was understandable, of course. Finally, after several months of badgering, the literary agent Zoë ffrench-Batistuta had agreed to a meeting. Today's lunch might well mark the beginning of a bright future. It might.

Mary had already downed four drinks and a packet of nuts. She was feeling a little squiffy and hoped it didn't show too much. Writers, she imagined, were sober, serious types. It wouldn't do to make the wrong impression. This was a business, not a hobby after all. She would need to appear calm, collected, with maybe just a hint of creative eccentricity. Undiscovered genius she might be, but she would need to demonstrate that she could interact with the real world. It was a chore, a huge pressure, but hell – vicars and nuns could do it, so why not?

She was sweating. It was particularly irritating in the region of her crotch. Her new sex organs contained a number of inverted sweat glands, which helped generate a useful amount of lube, but were a bugger in the comfort stakes. She wanted to scratch herself, but whereas the process had once required little more than a quick pinch and a rub, it was now invasive and frankly obscene. Maybe she should go to the loo and insert a medicated tampon. She always enjoyed that, though she had to leave herself little notes as reminders to take them out again. Sometimes the string got lost. She'd heard tales of women dying from tampon infections. Men really didn't know how lucky they were, poor non-bleeding things.

Zoë appeared finally, only half-an-hour late. She was carrying a bundle of papers in one hand, a pint in the other. It was exciting, to see a professional clutching Mary's manuscript in such a business-like fashion.

Zoë ffrench-Batistuta was a woman of profoundly limited talent. As a young girl she had felt most at home at the gymkhana. Schooling authors seemed a natural progression from keeping ponies. She took great delight in their cute mannerisms and wilful bouts of sulkiness. They were all like in-season mares, even the men. Especially the men, who were probably all gay.

She dreamed of spotting a great work, of being mentioned in glowing terms at an awards dinner. She dreamed of getting into film, of meeting 'A-list' celebs. In reality, she had more chance of shagging the Pope. She knew this, on a less superficial level. It made her a close friend of Prozac, and alcohol. She kept a bottle of vodka in the left-hand drawer of her desk, a bottle of port in the other. She also had a secret compartment, which she kept topped up with Special Brew. She liked to indulge her uncouth side sometimes, usually when she had her period. Nothing brought out the trucker-fucker in her like a parachuting egg.

It was all a little unfair, really. She worked twice as hard as her husband, the art historian Simon. She had changed her name to his not out of duty, but rather because she thought it might give her some advantage. Fat chance. Out of the two of them, he was the one who continued to attract all the plaudits. He had already popped up on the *South Bank Show*. He was on first name terms with Melvyn. He received an annual Christmas card from Damien. He knew people. Important people. He had a lazy eye, as if he had seen some terrible things at prep school, which had latterly caused his sense organs to lose interest. There was that about him which conveyed a sense of mystery. Bastard.

Zoë had recently relocated the office away from darkest Yorkshire, setting up camp in Atlantic Cornwall. This was partly due to Simon getting a position at the local branch of the Tate, partly because she thought the South-West might prove a more fertile hunting ground. All the great, undiscovered writers hung out in Cornwall. Everyone knew that. True, the St Ives postcode was a little embarrassing, from a professional point-of-view, but not everyone could afford to live in London. Maybe she would set a trend. She had website (which had already received seven hits) and liked to think she was fostering a reputation as an innovator.

So far she'd secured deals for two books. A small number in three years, admittedly, but she could take comfort in the fact that she was dealing in quality, not tat. One was entitled *'Drinking from the Furry Fountain: a Lesbian's Guide to Wine'*, the other dealt with the sensitive issue of homosexual pets. The latter was doing big numbers in the American Bible Belt, where gay pooches were a real problem.

Mary waved. Zoë nodded, then made her way across the terrace. She looked like a woman who knew everyone worth knowing, who slept with heads of major publishing houses, who had real, undeniable influence. This was the true art of the agent, giving head in return for a nice fat contract. Well worth 15 per cent of anyone's money. Mary would gladly have paid three times that figure if only she might get a book deal.

Zoë sat down at the table and instantly turned into a midget. Mary stared. "All my height's in my legs," Zoë apologised. "I have a very short torso, you see. Would probably look pretty crappy in a wheelchair, ha ha."

"Oh," Mary murmured. "Paraplegia is terrible, isn't it? I hope it never happens to me."

Mary hated herself for a moment.

"Yes," Zoë agreed anyway. "I know what you mean. I try to avoid sitting down wherever possible. It puts me at a disadvantage."

"I think they are very brave," Mary suggested. "Paraplegics, I mean."

Shut up, shut up!

Zoë gave the matter the attention it clearly didn't deserve. "Oh, I'm not sure they have much option, do they? Anyway, back in a mo. Need a wee."

Mary watched her leave, not quite sure what to think.

"Mary, hello," a beautiful voice said from behind her.

Mary span to see she was being watched by Sylvia Carey. The beautiful, naturally buxom, thin-armed, narrow-wasted, flared-hipped, perfect role-model Sylvia Carey. Oh, and she was clever and talented, of course. She was an artist.

"Hi," Mary acknowledged, her shock at being thus accosted conveying a wholly false sense of nonchalance.

"Can I join you?" Sylvia asked.

"Well, not really," Mary answered, though it caused her a good deal of pain to say it. "I'm meeting someone, you see. My agent."

"Oh good," Sylvia enthused, warmly. "Is that it? Is that your book?" She reached out, her fingers caressing the stack of papers. "Can I have a read?"

"No!"

"Bit saucy, is it?"

"It's not that," Mary replied. "It's just, well, you know-"

"Sooner or later everyone's going to read it, Mary. So where's the harm?"

"I'd rather you didn't, Sylvia. Not just yet. It's not finished."

"These things never are, in my experience. If I ever stumble across one of my old paintings, there are always things I'd change. But you have to draw the line somewhere."

"Oh, that's very clever!" Mary gushed, then immediately wished she hadn't.

Sylvia blinked. "Is it? Well, the thing is, you have to move on." She took a pointed breath. Things gathered deep in her chest. "You know, I was thinking. How your, ah, situation must put you at an advantage."

"Oh?"

"We women are always criticising male authors for their inability to create believable female characters, aren't we? Well, I'm assured the opposite also holds true. A woman can no more understand the mind of a man than a man can understand, well, anything really. The two states are quite alien. But you know how it feels to be a man. You also know how it feels to be a woman."

"I'm not sure I fully understand either condition," Mary admitted.

"Well, then at least your writing will have balance!"

Zoë appeared, just in time. She gawped as she saw Sylvia, who was obviously something of a star in the local arts world.

"Ms. Carey!"

"Mrs. Carey," Sylvia corrected with atypical vehemence. "Do I look like a lesbian?"

"Mrs. Carey!"

"Hello," Sylvia purred. "You must be the agent."

"Yes," Zoë confirmed. "Yes, yes! Zoë ffrench-Batistuta. Mrs. I believe you know my husband?"

"Simon? Indeed I do. Terrible man. Very pompous. Always winking."

"He has a lazy eye," Zoë murmured. And then, with a conspiratorial dip of her head, "He went to Harrow, you see."

Sylvia shrugged. "He's still an idiot."

"Oh yes," Zoë agreed readily. "Very much so. Anyway, as you say, I'm a literary agent. I represent people. I, well, you know-"

Sylvia smiled gently and the hard edge left her. "Have you any experience of working in film?" she asked, for no reason that was immediately apparent.

Zoe's eyes went so wide they looked momentarily piscine. "Film?" she whispered.

"Yes," Sylvia expanded. "I have a little project and I might need some expert advice. Could you spare a few minutes?"

"Now?"

Sylvia turned her head a fraction. "You don't mind, do you Mary?"

"Oh, no," Mary answered. "Why would I, in fact?"

She watched as the two conspirators retreated to the opposite side of the terrace. She cast her eyes inwards, into the pot of bile that lurked in the centre of her stomach. It was on the boil. Nicely on the boil.

Mary considered herself a remarkably placid person, usually – but there were times when she found herself thinking dark thoughts. Right now, she had a vision of a medieval torture chamber. Owen was there, acting as chief torturer. Mary would supply him with suitable candidates and he would oblige her as best he could. Rats, damp, mildew, blood, agony. She put her fingers to her ears, the sounds of protracted screaming almost splitting her head in two.

The Remarkable Everyday

****

Later that afternoon, she caught the train to Penzance where she had an appointment with her plastic surgeon, Dr Alleyne. Part of her was excited at the thought of meeting her saviour again; the other part wished that he could just leave her be. He insisted on regular post-operative consultations, taking a number of measurements and wot-not for his database. He had a dream, of constructing the perfect vagina, a study in ergonomic excellence, a sort of BMW Five-Series of the fanny world. Mary's procedure, stunning as it was, was merely a step towards that goal. She understood this, but did not mind. It was quite an uplifting thought, to consider that her occasional agonies might bring hope to men (and women) the world over.

The secretary brought her coffee and biscuits, which she sipped and nibbled demurely. Estelle was a lovely girl, really, very kind and supportive. Much nicer than Sylvia or Zoë, surely. The heroine in Mary's novel was constructed along similar lines. Estelle doubtless had a boyfriend who played cricket. Mary liked men who played cricket. Said a lot about a man's character that he should have the patience to chase a little ball of leather around a field for hours at a time. She imagined Owen dressed in whites. Hmmnn.

Mary daydreamed a little harder. Owen. Her first potential suitor! She was feeling a little nervous about their forthcoming rendezvous. She knew how men's minds worked. They were only after one thing. Or two, perhaps, if the Premiership title were taken into account.

Ah, but this was Cornwall, and they didn't have football down here. They had cliffs and gazing out at the sea. Mary congratulated herself on her choice of rendezvous point. It would be very romantic.

As a proper woman, Mary liked to gloss her carnal desires with a lippy of romance. It was all a lie, of course. All she really wanted was to touch his cock.

In that respect, she was looking forward to seeing things from the other side of the genital divide. Her own todger had been possessed of a wilful, somewhat malevolent sense of independence. It had been like a vampire, sucking blood from her body to feed its peculiar hunger for things she did not understand. A parasite.

As a woman, Mary felt compelled to subscribe to the standard female view of all things phallic – they were clearly ridiculously shaped and ugly as only inflatable flesh can be. To be fair, though, a flower shaped – for instance – object would never have worked, in a penetrative sense. Maybe – gasp! – it was all the fault of the vagina.

Speaking of which, she was finally shown into Dr Alleyne's office. The doctor looked up as she entered, smiling his familiar greeting. Mary smiled back. It was all right. No emotional baggage. Just two old friends meeting after a few weeks apart. Perfectly normal. They would have a perfectly normal conversation, perhaps share the odd anecdote-

"Right, let's have a look at your vagina," Dr Alleyne said.

Mary found herself slipping into the old apparatus, a shiny mass of pulleys, levers and stirrups, which might have sent a medieval torturer into an ecstasy of professional delight. Despite the relative warmth of the day, every surface was freezing cold.

"Any problems?" Alleyne enquired from somewhere between her legs. His words were curiously reverberative, as if he were speaking into the mouth of a large cave. Mary did not know whether to feel embarrassed at the implication of volume or rather listen out for the echo.

"Well, not really," she answered.

"Not really?"

"It's still a bit itchy," she admitted. "Actually, it's quite a lot itchy. Seems to be getting a bit worse, in fact. I've been taking the pills, but-"

"Hmm."

"Can you see anything doctor? Is everything all right?"

Dr Alleyne's head reappeared over the parapet of Mary's knees. He scratched thoughtfully at his chin. "Bit inflamed, in places," he replied. "Doesn't look like a STD, or anything like that. Now I don't want to alarm you unduly, Mary, but we might have to face up to the possibility of rejection."

"Rejection? You mean my body is rejecting my vagina? How can that be?"

"Well, there's always a risk."

"But only if you take grafts from someone else, surely."

"Well, funny you should mention that."

Mary sat upright, struggling to free herself from the restraints. "You didn't," she whispered. "You said you weren't going to."

"I had a problem with the labia minora," Alleyne said with a shrug. "I happened to have some material lying around, so-"

"Material? You weren't making curtains, doctor!"

"Mary, Mary, you misunderstand. This was a state-of-the-art procedure. I was very thorough. The risk of rejection fell within acceptable limits."

"Shit. What am I going to do? I mean, I'm sure I could get by without an arm, or a leg, but – excuse me – a vagina? Isn't it kind of imperative?"

"Not really," Alleyne answered smoothly. "One hole's as good as the next, if you want to be brutal about it. All the twirly bits are more decorative than functional. We'll give you a rebore, if necessary."

"I am not an engine, either!" And then she bit her lip

because a proper woman should not know anything about internal combustion and the repair of damaged cylinder liners.

"Well, it's not that bad yet. I'm going to prescribe you a few goodies that might help. All being well, things will settle down again fairly soon."

"And if they don't?"

"Then we have another go, I suppose."

"Oh, Lord," Mary groaned as she pulled up her knickers. "Why is nothing ever simple? Do they have any side-effects, these new pills?"

"Well, you might notice the odd mood swing. The odd flash of violent psychosis. Quite normal for a female, I should say."

"Tell me. Whose labia am I carrying around inside me?"

"Oh, I don't recall exactly. A Chinese girl, I think. A student, perhaps. I do remember that she was run over outside B&Q, if that's of any use to you."

"I've got a mixed race vagina," was all Mary could think to say. "My mother is probably turning in her grave."

Mary stomped out of the surgery, thumping along the street towards the station. By the time she arrived home, she was still furious. Why was the world such a nasty, complicated place? The odds on it existing at all were as near as dammit one in infinity, so adding a little measure of contentment would hardly have been placing an unnecessary strain on the laws of probability.

She looked around for something to break. Aha! She seized hold of her sketch and in a fit of further temper proceeded to obliterate Sylvia's image from the canvass. Traitress!

Afterwards, she located Fraggle and gave him a vigorous stroking. The old moggy seemed oblivious to her mood; he yawned, farted, then settled down for a snooze. A lap was a lap to his way of thinking, however it was presented.

Mary took a deep breath and rather irresponsibly focused all of her hope on Owen. She did not know what she would do if the date did not go well.

****

The seal was in a sorry state. It looked up as they approached, flapping a flipper dejectedly. Some gunky substance oozed out from one eye, the other was shut tight. It made a peculiar honking sound, as if calling to its more fortunate fellows out at sea. One or two of these, their whiskered noses silhouetted against the dark splodge of Godrevy Island, looked on as the scene unfolded, their soft faces a study in melancholy. They were relatively common around the coast – but not so common that a death or injury went unnoticed among their own kind.

And nothing is as sad in life as a grieving seal, except maybe a lonely whale. It's in the eyes.

"Well I never," Mary murmured. "Who'd have thought-"

"Happens all the time," Owen said as he dropped down by the injured creature. "Daft buggers are always crashin' into the rocks. There's some bastard currents out there, mind."

"What's wrong with him?"

"It's a her," Owen replied. "Can't you tell the difference?"

"Oh, of course," Mary answered blandly.

Owen stroked his hand along the seal's back. She had all but dried out and felt surprisingly furry.

"Shush," he said as the seal attempted to flop away. "We'll get you some help, yeah? You gotta mobile, Mary?"

Mary handed Owen her phone. She watched as he tapped in the number, his slender fingers a blur over the keypad. He looked almost beautiful, what with his long, reddy-gold hair wrapping itself around his delicate features. Quite like a girl.

Did that make her a lesbian? Whatever, he made her feel awkward, boyish.

"Fag?" Owen offered as he handed the phone back.

"No, thanks. Who did you call?"

"RSPCA. They'll be here in a quarter-of-an-hour."

"You know the number off by heart?"

"I've got some nasty friends."

Mary sat down next to him. She patted the seal, feeling a bit awkward about it. It was helpless, like a baby. Babies made her feel nervous. She was afraid of anything that seemed less in control of its circumstances than she was of her own.

That had been formed in a womb. Mary had no womb. In her lighter moments, she fantasised that she'd had a hysterectomy.

Childbirth. Everything about it scared her. Made her a little envious, too, because the things that still made her different from other women, those anatomical hotspots, were rooted in procreation. Her hips, particularly, were a source of disappointment, designed as they were to expedite the basic process of running after a wild boar, or playing football, and nothing more. The female pelvis, of course, has a dual function. It also has nowhere to go, in evolutionary terms. Any more flared and a woman wouldn't be able to walk. So human children are all born several months premature, even those that are carried the full term. If the gestation period were any longer, our huge-brained progeny wouldn't fit through the birth canal. This is why human babies are so helpless when compared to, say, a newborn deer.

This was perhaps Mary's favourite fact. It always amazed her that other women didn't find it equally interesting.

Out at sea, a single shaft of yellow light was leaking through the clouds as if God, or some other drunken deity, were taking a piss. It was a beautiful, if slightly chilly, place to spend an evening. She shivered, crossing her legs to shut out the breeze that whistled up her skirt.

Owen wrapped an arm around her shoulders. She still felt a little uncomfortable, to be touched in such a provocative fashion by a teenager, but not so uncomfortable that she could bring herself to push him away. She had waited twenty years to feel this, ever since puberty had set her off into an emotional and physical cul-de-sac. She had to lean into him a little, to make the angles more comfortable. Owen was barely five-four. Mary herself was five-eight. He was seventeen, she was thirty-three.

He had been born male, so had she.

There. They had something in common. Mary closed her eyes and tried to think calming thoughts. She was as new to all this as he was. It wasn't as if she was taking advantage of him, after all.

No, look at him. See the mischievous look in his eye as he spots a chance to satisfy an urge. He wants this. How typically male he is. His curiosity, his artless manoeuvring, so transparent, is a powerful aphrodisiac.

She edged a little closer. He had a peculiar smell about him, which again was stimulating. She rested her hand on his thigh. His hand sunk a little lower, an inch at a time, until he had her breast. She let out a little sigh, like a woman was supposed to. It felt nice, to have someone else doing the caressing for a change. Owen didn't seem to care much about her unconventional route to sexual maturity, so why should she? And so what if her breasts were a little firmer than they should have been? Plenty of real women chose to give nature a helping hand.

She stooped her head, until her lips brushed his. It was easier this time. His fingers trembled against the faint scar, where they had broken and reset her jaw into a softer shape.

She could feel his strength, out of proportion with his refugee skinniness. She felt a gratifying sense of danger, as if at any moment he could pin her down and ravage her. They were miles away from anywhere, with only an injured seal to act as a chaperone.

The reality was that she still retained the remnants of her old male strength. She despised it, longed for the day she would have to ask a man to open a bottle of sauce for her. She was getting a little weaker, a little bit more vulnerable each day. But it wasn't happening quickly enough. It was stupid, but she needed to feel the full range of what it meant to be a woman, even if that meant exposing herself to danger. She needed the full, unequivocal experience.

She kissed him again. His fingers found a way inside her dress, and into her bra. She was a C-cup, which seemed a nice size to be. Not as spectacularly proportioned as Sylvia, right enough, but still nice. Very normal. Not gratuitous, yet still a good handful. Enough to draw admiring glances from men, not so much as to arouse the scorn of other women. They were surprisingly heavy, surprisingly unwieldy, but she loved them all the same. She would run her fingers between them for hours at a time, over and around them, her mind racing away on romantic visions of plunging necklines, and heaving bosoms. It was a joyous feeling, to find herself in such a condition, like a gospel choir had taken up residence inside her head.

And then his hand went down below. She held her breath, fearing that he might be disgusted.

But no, think positively! For all the slight possibility of rejection, the doctors had done a wonderful job; they had assured her that she was, cosmetically speaking, as convincing as any other woman. And it certainly felt wonderful, all the old nerve endings firing in response to his touch. And to think it was basically a penis turned inside out. Remarkable. She groaned again, spreading her legs a little wider as his finger snagged accidentally against her clitoris. Her clit was best of all – a work of art. Dr Alleyne said it was his greatest achievement. He had even taken pictures of it that he might use in a new brochure. Just think of that – her clit on posters in sex clinics all over the country, and beyond. Dr Alleyne had a growing reputation in the States, too.

Perhaps he might even ask Mary to accompany him to a conference. Mary O'Connor, international clitoral superstar!

It had all been worth it. All the drugs, the vomiting, the pain, the self-disgust. Cutting her rectum with a knife so the blood would drip into the toilet bowl like a period. Staring at herself for hours in the mirror, crying at her gratuitous muscularity and hideous, distended Adam's apple. All these had been steps on the parabolic curve of self-discovery.

Yes, she thought in curves now, rather than straight lines. Perfect, sweeping, grand-romantic curves.

Things were interrupted by the arrival of the RSPCA man. He raised one eyebrow at the sight of the unlikely couple, so obviously mussed, but did not pass comment. Mary looked at him defiantly, daring him to say anything. She could feel her surgically enhanced nipples stand out stiff through her dress and half-hoped the man didn't notice. Only half, mind you.

Owen stared at his feet, cheeks flaming, which Mary found surprisingly hurtful. Ashamed of being with her, was he? Maybe it was just the bashfulness of youth. Yes, that was undoubtedly it. Owen would have blushed whoever he was caught with.

They helped the uniformed man load the seal onto a stretcher. The poor creature honked, its gammy eye emitting a stream of liquid.

"It's not crying, is it?" Mary asked, girl-like.

The RSPCA man sniffed and climbed back into his van. Like many of his type, the love and kindness had long since left him. If you've seen one tortured animal, Mary supposed, you've seen a thousand. It was even worse with doctors, though not, strangely, plastic surgeons.

He trundled off, his expression clearly visible in the rear-view mirror. It was not disgust, as Mary would have anticipated, rather it was something that contained an element of lust. She could not make up her mind how this made her feel. As ever, everything was rather ambiguous.

But this was good. Very natural. It was her duty to feel offended if men did stare at her, and offended if they did not. Perhaps she should get one of those t-shirts with writing in the breast area, 'what are you looking at?' or something like that. She giggled to herself as she considered all the possibilities for making mischief.

She took station behind Owen. He really was rather adorable. She reached around his waist, her fingers trembling over his groin. It was beautiful, with the sea crashing around them, as if it were applauding their kind deed. It made her feel good about herself. A perfect day to consider whether she might wish to give up her virginity. Dr. Alleyne had even created an artificial hymen for her. She could feel it now, vibrating like a timpani inside her. Sometimes she had nightmares, that it wouldn't break when required, that it would exist as a permanent barrier to further pleasure. But right now those fears seemed a long way behind her. She was confident, relaxed.

"Let's move on," Owen muttered, his strange tone breaking the mood in an instant.

"Oh. Okay, then."

She offered her hand, but he ignored it. They walked in silence, up the steps from the spit, up into the tufty grass on the top of the cliff, past the ice-cream van with its sad-looking one-armed attendant, past the balloon seller, who looked sadder still. The balloons were shrunken in the chill breeze, saggy and contracted like an old woman's breasts. Mary's would never sag. Even when old and battered, when every other part of her had given way, her baps would remain, firm and proud, a reminder of what she had been.

Owen didn't seem much aware of his surroundings. He rather deliberately walked a yard to the left of her, his face a study in neutrality. He still had the erection, though. Mary watched it out of the corner of her eye, covetous.

They passed a couple of teenage girls, maybe Owen's age. One, a pretty young thing with pigtails, grinned as she saw Owen's hard-on. Mary wanted to shout, "it's mine!" but somehow managed to restrain herself. The girls passed by, giggling and whispering. Owen didn't seem to notice them at all. Why would he, though? He was with her, no one else.

They came finally to the edge of the world. Out at sea, cargo ships glistened. Closer in, fishing boats took station over secret hordes of fish. Nearer still, a middle-aged man was flying a kite. It flashed in the weak sun, diving like a falcon into the abyss, before reappearing in a billowing flutter of plastic. The man watched it, sadly, his melancholy clinging like mist to his anorak. No happy, stable person would ever choose such a hobby, where every flight ends in death. No good ever comes of it.

"See them rocks down there?" Owen said.

"What, those big ones just beneath the water?"

"That's them. Do you know how they got there?"

"No."

"A giant threw 'em there."

"Why would he do that?"

"He was aiming at passing ships. He was called Ralph and

he lived in a cupboard. That's what his cave was called. The Cupboard. Anyway, he would sink the ships and take them back to his cave to eat the sailors."

"How dreadful! I-"

Her mobile rang, the shock of the artificial, monophonic noise making her start. She fiddled with it, forgetting, as ever, which key accepted the call. "Hello? Hello? Oh, nuts. Ah. Hello?"

"I've seen your advert in the phone box," a husky voice said down the line. "Is it true? Can you fuck yourself up your own fanny?"

"Oh, piss off," Mary replied. She switched the phone off, carefully stowing it away in her handbag. "Fucking Billy London," she cursed. "I thought I'd found all those bloody posters."

When she looked up, Owen was staring at her.

"Why did you come to St Ives?" he asked.

"Oh. To write my novel, mainly."

"Why here, though? Why not Penzance, or Zennor?"

"My uncle left me his cottage." She looked out to sea. "Which was rather fortuitous. If ever I'm going to find inspiration, then it'll be here."

Owen lapsed into a contemplative silence. "What's it like?" he asked eventually. "Bein' a woman, I mean."

"Difficult," Mary answered. "But probably less difficult than being a man. I didn't realise, before, how easy we – women, I mean – get it. Did you know that the male suicide rate is ten times higher than the female one? I used to think about it all the time, you know. But not any more. Yes, it's very hard being a man. I don't think women think about that, sometimes. We're closeted really. Or do I mean cosseted?"

"Whatever. And you like that, being protected?"

"I do," Mary answered. "I like it when a man gives up his

seat for me on the bus. I like it when he holds a door open for me. It makes me feel valued."

"I held a door open for a lady once," Owen mused. "She looked at me like I was a right asshole. Said she was quite capable of doin' it fur erself. I've not much bothered with all that stuff since."

"Well, that's a shame. Don't let it put you off."

"Why'd ya do it, though? Not sure cutting me cock off would make me happy."

"It wasn't like that. It felt wrong, before."

"And now?"

"And now it feels better."

"Well, yur lookin' good, anyway."

Mary bowed her head in acknowledgment of the compliment, then sat down on the grass. Owen joined her, albeit a bit hesitantly. The kite flying man turned to look at them, one eyebrow raised quizzically, before turning back to his lonely pursuit. Owen sighed, his fingers tearing strips from the mossy grass.

"Does my past make you feel uncomfortable?" Mary asked stiffly.

She held her breath, dreading the response. He frowned, his expressive face revealing a whole host of complex emotions.

"All girls make me feel uncomfortable," he said.

Somehow, this was the nicest thing he could possibly have said to her. She reached out to take his hand and this time he didn't push it away.

Wednesday

By
E.C.Seaman

The Remarkable Everyday

Sweetheart, take a tip from one who knows. If you're going to end this, and I mean really carry it off, not just make a feeble attempt, or a cry for help, then please, don't do it in the bath. I know it does sound like a soothing, easy way out, sanitised and quite civilised; it's what the Romans used to do after all, a sharp knife, a spurt of blood and a gentle candlelit slipping away into oblivion in warm, scented water. But no, I beg of you, retain for yourself some dignity in death. Just imagine if the films and books are true, if there is an afterlife and we're trapped there just as we were at the point of passing, then surely you'll spend eternity naked as the day you were born, but white, bloated and wet.

I've really studied this you know, evaluated every way to end the charade. I've made plans, researched my subject more thoroughly than Dorothy Parker ever did. I've tested the tip of a kitchen knife against the bare, creamy flesh of my inner arm, traced the fine blue threads of blood beneath the skin. She may have listed the various ways and means, and neat objections against each method, but anyone who makes suicide merge into poetry is not taking the subject seriously enough. And I understand as well that the wistful Sixties' song was wrong – suicide isn't painless, but it surely is aimless. But then, aimlessness sums up so much of what we do together.

I used to believe all our problems were just that old Mars versus Venus thing. I dignified all our early rows with the wonderfully romantic catch-all cliché: it's an attraction of opposites. What total crap. Remember that college friend of ours who fell frantically in love with a Spanish girl, though they didn't speak a word of each other's language, at least at first. We marvelled at it, intrigued as if a hippo and a giraffe had mated. How bizarre, we laughed; how do they communicate, we wondered. But you and I speak the same language and, after all these years, we still can't understand one another. Maybe your brain's wired differently to mine, or you learnt a different form of speech. Perhaps when I say 'love', you hear 'hate'. Or do you hear something even less relevant, a random word like 'lawnmower' or 'fruit'? When I talk about emotions, I think it must sound to you like overhearing someone speaking Dutch, the words are faintly familiar, but have wrong, unexpected, disturbing meanings.

You can generalise our differences in any way you like, it makes no difference; we're at completely different ends of the emotional spectrum and have found no way of reaching across to each other. At first I devoured glossy magazines for tips on how to deal with you and believed that all we needed was interests in common. Their agony aunts instructed me that love thrives in a household when there's a shared love of long walks or French films, Mexican food or body piercing. Well, that's all very well, but really so superficial. It's a shared attitude to arguments that you really need.

Now your philosophy, if I can call it that, is simple – you always feel the best way through a problem is to avoid it altogether. But surely that's like evading bills until the bailiff comes to hammer down the door, or ignoring the silent seep of gas until one carelessly lit cigarette blows the whole house to ashes. You just brush it all under the carpet and keep sweeping away until the accumulated rubbish makes the floor rise in steep impassable ridges, like the Himalayas.

I, in contrast, come from a long line of theatrical types. We love to let it all hang out. I have a proud genetic heritage of operatic rows, of crockery smashing plate-flingers who argue dramatically, regularly, at the top of their voices. It may be loud and momentarily frightening, but then like a summer storm it all blows over, leaving the air clean and refreshed. Nothing is hidden, our dirty linen is laundered, starched and hung out to dry in public. But nothing festers, nobody sulks, there are no guilty secrets.

Why wallow in it? You say, brow furrowed, why dwell on the past? All the pain will go away if you think about something, anything, else. Except that little ruse doesn't work indefinitely. Eventually the hurt and fear and loneliness come bursting out, mutated into venomous anger. Wounds may look healed on the surface, sealed over with tender pink new flesh, but underneath the same old emotions suppurate and squirm like maggots, turned hateful and rotten. Our differences feel like a lesion I have to keep scratching at, a splinter lodged deep in my soul. It will fester until the bad parts are dug out, until the infection's finally cut from my body.

I've always tried to prove to myself that you're not inhuman, as I have sometimes had reason to suspect through long dark nights spent tear-drenching the spare bed. Maybe, I rationalise, you simply need to be taught how to love. Your blankness isn't a lack of feeling, just a careful defence, hard knocks have given you a stiff upper lip that just needs to be kissed into tenderness. And so I've always hoped to make that one bold gesture that will eventually crack your reserve, make you fling your arms around me and say you love me, that will finally force you to feel. But every time I pour my heart out to you, I receive no passionate response, just that blank look, a raised eyebrow. Those are the weapons you use, not fists or feet or angry words. Instead you wield silence, a change of subject, stiff and resentful one-armed hugs, politely gritted teeth.

Maybe this is why I have so frequently fantasised about accidents. You must be careful what you wish for, so obviously nothing too painful. No long-term health risks or disfigurement, nothing sordid, nothing irreversible. Just enough to provoke a reaction from you. Maybe I'd leap from the sea wall into stormy waves to pluck a winsome child from certain death. But somehow, after the rescue, I'd fall myself and become a heroine in the process.

I dream of you waiting patiently by my hospital bedside, praying for me to wake. You're pale from lack of sleep, gently tearing your hair, tears running down your face. You plead with me to wake because you love me too much to ever contemplate losing me. And then (miraculously thinner and rather more beautiful than in reality) I start to stir. Unfeasibly long eyelashes flutter gently on my rose-petal cheeks, and I open my eyes to see you looking tenderly down at me. The music swells as we kiss, passionately. Fade out to credits. The only time I was really in hospital, groggy and irritable with morphine, I was punctured with so many drips, tubes and leads connected to bleeping monitors that a kiss would have been a practical impossibility. Still, it's a good fantasy.

In our beginning, they say, is our end. And somehow, even as we began, I knew there would be no happy ending. One summer's evening, not long after we started, we went to a party with some of your more glamorous friends. The girls flocked round you, sweetened by clouds of scent, laughing, fluttering up at you. The evening darkened, the ground shifting beneath my feet. I was suddenly nauseated, afraid. Why hadn't I noticed this before? I realised, sickened, that I'd finally caught the bug and was undeniably in love.

I was so scared of those shimmering girls, that I couldn't compete, that their fevered glances would melt you. I fled to the bedroom to cry hot, mortified tears. Then a vicious, low-voiced row, sharp words, angry accusations. I threw a glass of white wine over the crotch of your pale jeans. It looked as if you'd wet yourself. Furious, you dragged me out of the house, stormed back through town, shoulders hunched, jacket pulled down to hide the spreading stain.

"I can't believe you bloody did that. I just don't understand this jealous rage in you."

You changed into clean clothes, made me go back to the party with you.

"I'm damned if I'm having everybody laugh behind my back. We're going back in there and you'll lift your chin, dry your face and behave as if nothing's happened." Humiliation. My face still burns hot at the thought, years later.

That night you relented, tried to smooth me down. Floods of tears, repentance. It took days before we could laugh normally again. Not a good start. And somehow, after that day, everything, even as we made love, or laughed together, or celebrated success, seemed to me to be subtly tinged with sadness, as if I'd seen the end and was already mourning. Can you feel loss before you've actually lost something?

Yet through it all, I've never stopped loving you – a real, wild, fierce love of hunger and possession. And I do believe you love me, as much as you can. Remember that sunny afternoon on the river? I'm poised on the edge of the boat, my shoes kicked off, toes curling round the sun-warmed wooden rail for balance, for leverage. You gasp, reach out a warning hand. Then, still fully clothed, I dive straight in. The water closes over my head, cool as green glass; the peace obliviates all memories. For several lifetimes I remain suspended underwater, luxuriating in the dark river silky against my skin. Then I rise to the surface, bubbling with laughter, and you're leaning over the side of the boat, aghast, amazed, admiring, aroused. But you can't have one kind of passion without the other. You want the free-spirited river nymph, but without all the darkness that drives my obsession. But extract that passion and what will be left of me?

You confided your fantasies; I was the first for you, for so many things. A half-embarrassed whisper that you'd really like to make love in the open air. The weekend finds us tumbling in a set-aside hayfield, the dusty grass-scent in my mouth as the clipped stalks prickle and tease at my back. You lie, exhausted, exhilarated, laughing up at the sun. I pop a strawberry into your mouth and you roll me over and over, giddy with your own daring. A cloud scuds across the sky, its shadow rolling towards us, darkening the fields as it passes over. The grass shivers and waves, rippling in a sudden chill of breeze. We scuffle our clothes on, barely decent before curious ramblers hurry by, trying not to stare. Red-faced at our lapse of taste, you bundle me back to the car. Life with you is sometimes no picnic, sweetheart.

And yet you're never cruel, only baffled. Your distance isn't deliberate. It's just you have the knack of making my most deep and heartfelt pleadings sound histrionic and forced, as if I'm a character in a bad soap opera. When we plunge inevitably into the same old grooves of argument, I feel I'm playing out a scripted drama in front of millions of viewers; our own little domestic melodrama three nights a week and repeated on Sundays. But then, you've always had the ability to make everything I say seem trite, hysterical, even when I'm being quite calm, for me. Because next to you, I am hysterical. I'm the stormy little Faeroes, rainlashed, riotous and wild. And you are vast, silent Alaska, calm, cool, composed and utterly bleak.

I remember standing in the kitchen, watching you make a bacon sandwich, a big ketchup-laced wedge, the way you always liked them. I was trying to explain how I feared losing you, how I was sure that one day I'd just find a note on the kitchen table to tell me you'd gone and that would be the end of it all. I waited for you to comment, to laugh, to brush aside my fears, hug me, whatever. You moved to the kettle and flicked it on.

"Do you want a cup of tea?" you asked, calmly.

Can you ever hope to pinpoint the moment when it all starts to fall away, to slide downhill?

How about one of those dreadful evenings with your colleagues? Pick any one – they merge together, indistinguishable in the memory, like a month of rainy Sundays. The habitual choice of venue is a secluded country hotel; the type with a hushed, silver-serviced, chintzily reverential air. My pre-dinner drink nervously turns into several stiff vodkas. The pianist playing elaborate, tinkling versions of TV show themes makes me giggle. Tail-coated waiters perform their synchronised silver dome-lift with a flourish and I laugh uncontrollably. The meal comes in pretentiously tiny portions, swirled with coulis, garnished with raspberry leaves. I can't find my own mouth with my fork and jab my cheek painfully with the prongs. Still not sobered enough, I attempt earnest conversation.

"She's not been well," I hear you whisper, as I sway back from the ladies room. "She really shouldn't drink with the medication she's on." They smile politely, catching each other's eyes, slyly unconvinced. Afterwards I try to explain how I can never relax with these people, always wary of their contempt – they don't think I'm good enough, they won't let me fit in. You turn away, uncomprehending, and I die a little.

But however I try and excuse it, I know this parting is ultimately my fault. I'm sorry, I really didn't mean for it to go so far. You've only come back today to make sure the house is sorted out before you sell it. And I know how much you loved this house, how you hate losing it like this. Your father's come with you for moral support; he looks right through me, still angry. I see the familiar clench of his jaw and, with a lurch of the heart, know that within a few years, when you start to grey, you will look just like him. And I realise that because I've lost you now, I won't be the one to watch you age, to catch the grey creeping into your hair, the lines deepening on your face. That hurts more than anything else that's passed between us. I always thought we'd be there for each other in our old age.

The memories come thick and fast, as if I'm witnessing every moment of our relationship, spooling out all at once. Now I can see you driving us down the motorway, stereo blaring so loud that the whole car vibrates. One of the thrashy bands you unexpectedly prefer, all testosterone angst and bumping bass guitar. I like this track though; the lyrics always strike a chord. 'Some day, somehow, I'm going to make it all right, but not right now'. I realised the first time I heard the song that it was how we had lived our lives for so many years, on the basis that one day we'd sit down and sort it all out. We knew it was wrong, but still we never managed to make the time.

Another day, not so long ago, I remember walking on the beach with you, fighting back the tears, biting down hard on the words that wanted to tumble from me like the waves falling spent on the rocky shore. Come on girl, I urged myself, don't start it all again, don't interrogate, don't ask for details. Just try to enjoy the sun on your face, the light on the waves, the sigh of the surf. But it's hard to walk with stones in your pockets and a lump in your throat, the tears blurring your eyes so that you stumble and fall. No sweetheart, it's okay; it's only the wind stinging my eyes that makes me cry. I didn't even try to explain and knew then that the end was very near.

I reach out a hand to you. Your face is so familiar, so beloved, but there are already lines I've never seen before; it must be this harsh morning light flooding through the bathroom window. You look so tired, my dear. I realise you can't see me, but still you shiver as my hand slides unseen through your cheek.

So I made you cry then, in the end, but it wasn't what I'd hoped for. You cried when you saw me there, lying in the red-stained bathwater, all the life leached out. But they were, above all, tears of fury that I'd finally done this thing, taken it to the limit. Silly cow. And even as you clutched me in your arms, tried to shake me alive, there was revulsion too, for this dead white thing that used to be your wife.

Today you'll take one last look around the house before you hand the keys to the estate agent and walk away. I want to call you back, to try and keep you here, but I know within minutes you'll leave and never come back. I can't ride out of here on your coat-tails, but remain, abandoned and alone, in the place we called home. The door shuts behind you and I hear your footsteps crunching away down the gravel path. I will never leave. I can never leave. I fall to the floor, but as mute as those old Roman ghosts, I cannot even cry out.

Friday

By
Brett Pransky

Nicholas and Betty Wheeler slept with their backs to each other, a king-sized ocean of mattress separating them. The habit began sometime in the fifth year of their marriage and continued for the next twelve, each passing year darkening the boundary line down the centre of the bed. As time passed, Nick and Betty – once famous for sneaking off into broom closets at parties whenever the mood and the wine intersected – now barely touched, each equally unwilling to venture into foreign and unfriendly waters. After seventeen years of marriage, sex had devolved into a thing for anniversaries and minor reconciliations. They only gave themselves to each other when the situation required it. Marriage had become a small scale Cold War with acts once done out of love now conducted as if by treaty, always in the centre of the bed, neither fully committing to the other's territory, each believing the other to be the enemy.

The flowing auburn hair, a wavy river of it, falling down over the delicate naked shoulders and perfect breasts of the woman in Nick's dream encounter, disappeared as the electronic whine of the alarm clock ushered in the morning. An increasing number of days were beginning this way, an unfaithful dream leaving Nick with equal portions of unfulfilled desire and undesired guilt. With a groan, which sounded too aged for his thirty-nine-year-old mouth, Nick reached out and backhanded the clock as he forced a weary body into an upright, but slouched, posture and reached out with his toes to the place where his slippers should have been.

Nick forgot that he had left his slippers next to his reading chair the night before, but the cold parquet floor reminded him as it stole the remaining grogginess and replaced it with a shiver. The Eighteenth Century Victorian home where he lived seemed to draw in the January cold rather than keep it out, hoarding the chill wind somewhere beneath the floorboards and dispensing it cruelly to unsuspecting toes. With eyes wide open, and without his fuzzy foot coverings, Nick stood and reached to the sky, shaking off the cold as he took the first steps of the day. In a familiar series of cracks and pops – the result of an athletic youth – Nick's ankles and knees went through their morning ritual as he stood, stretched, then waddled into the master bathroom.

'You're only as old as you feel', he thought as he scraped the new hair from his face with the old-fashioned double-sided razor given to him – along with a bottle of Old Spice aftershave – as a Christmas present from his then four-year-old daughter Emma. Now sixteen, she didn't speak to her father unless on command or out of necessity. Nick stopped issuing those commands a few months back and Emma needed him less with each passing day, so the jilted father decided to give in and let things take their natural course. He never spoke to his parents at sixteen either. *'She'll need money someday. Then she'll like me again.'*

This thought came as the last remnants of his stubble fell into the sink, with a few more grey bits among the mass than he would have liked. Opening the medicine cabinet, Nick instinctively reached for his Old Spice, then passed it over and settled on something a little more modern, a blue bottle with a French name he didn't know the meaning of. A few painful taps on each cheek and then a quick inspection of the hair just above his ears – looking for more grey shards and finding too many. Nick now felt ready to begin the day. He took one last look at himself, the trimmed but full, dark brown hair, peppered at the edges, the serious blue eyes just beginning to show the bags of age, and the small arched creases extending from the corners of his nose to his chin, framing his mouth. Age was winning the struggle, but slowly. *'You're only as old as you feel.'*

After shuffling through his array of sport coats and khaki slacks, Nick decided on a pair of navy blue trousers and a grey jacket he had purchased about a month before on the advice of a friend. He completed his attire with a tie given to him for his last birthday by his silent child. He hadn't gained much weight through the years so his waistline had never forced him into updating his wardrobe. As a result of his static mass, combined with his hatred for all things retail, most of Nick's clothing was painfully outdated. But, for a university English professor, this was pretty much the status quo. Smart people were not supposed to be concerned with clothing. They were supposed to be concentrating on the progression of knowledge. A stylish professor was one who either had a stylish wife or one who neglected his scholarly duties. Until recently, Nick followed this model, even, from time to time, donning a brown tweed jacket with leather patches over the elbows, known in professorial circles as the fashion shibboleth of the learned. But not today. Today he looked like a businessman, like a man moving up in the world. *'Someone going somewhere.'* Once he buttoned, tied, and properly belted and shoed himself, Nick started towards the stairs on his way to the kitchen, where breakfast always waited.

As if the sound of feet on the steps were a cue in a Broadway play, Emma rose from her seat and bolted for the door, leaving a half-eaten piece of toast and still-warm eggs on her plate. Before Nick could get the words, "Have a nice day", out of his mouth, the door closed with Emma on the outside, on her way to school in the car he had bought for her, without so much as a "Good morning, Daddy" for his trouble. Instead of going to the kitchen, Nick stepped to the window to watch her leave. Emma's sandy blonde hair, cut just above her shoulders – like her mother's once was – danced back and forth across her face as she looked up and

66

down the street before backing out of the stone driveway. *'Just like her mother.'*

"Would you like some coffee, Nick?"

"Huh?"

"I'll get you a cup." Nick was still partly immersed in the daydream, too caught up admiring the past to listen to the tedious questions of the present. As Emma's car sped away, at a velocity Nick was not comfortable with, and vanished into the white backdrop, he found his eyes moving to the treetops. A gentle wind, unusual at that time of year, flowed among the high leafless branches, making them weave in and out of each other as if dancing, like many hands lifted in celebration or innumerable prayers raised to Heaven, calling out for the Spring and its new life. *'Is that what they want? A new life?'*

"I brought in the paper for you," Betty interrupted. Her words felt somehow blasphemous, like a giggle during Mass or an unremoved hat during the national anthem at a sporting event.

"I'll be right there," he replied. Nick turned to see his wife passing through the kitchen doorway on her way to attend to a sink full of breakfast dishes. She wore a full-length house-coat made of a dull, blue terrycloth, a far cry from the pink satin of their first years together. Back then the robes were shorter and tied loosely, often exposing her ample bosom and leading to morning sex on the very table where his coffee now sat cooling. They used to joke about the probability of their daughter having been conceived on that table, and also about the hours Betty spent scrubbing egg and coffee stains out of the delicate pink fabric.

Nick bought her several new robes during the first year, a few less the year after, and so on and so on, until she no longer wore them, which happened at a time he couldn't remember now. What was once meant to tease and seduce had become a tool used to cover and hide. Betty's figure had grown over the years, not quick like the irresponsible, fast-food chomping masses, but gradually, like the concentric rings of a slow-growing tree, the natural change that occurs in all men and women. She was still quite attractive for her age, but time and familiarity had doused the sexual fire of the relationship many years before, leaving a once desired wife self-conscious and semi-depressed. She turned to the traditional role of mother and homemaker for solace, as if excelling at these could somehow validate her sexless role in the marriage. Now she looked the part, from the frumpy slippers to the robe, to the chopped locks of blonde hair that were now easier to manage.

Nick slid into his usual spot at the head of the small kitchen table and picked up his copy of *The Dispatch*, just as he had every morning for as long as he cared to remember. But before he could begin his reading, Betty was at him again, chirping about some present thing that couldn't possibly be important. Nick did as he usually did when he wanted to be left alone; he ignored her and unfolded the paper, holding it up in front of him as a shield against the monotony. Usually, after a few seconds, the noise would stop, followed by a small sigh. But this was different. She wasn't taking no for an answer. Right in the middle of an article on the upcoming school board elections, *The Dispatch* simply disappeared. Nick felt as if he had witnessed a magic trick, like someone had just snatched a tablecloth from under a full set of dishes. He would have been impressed if he wasn't so annoyed. "What do you want?"

"I need to talk to you," Betty said. Nick started to get up from his chair. He smelled confrontation and he wanted no part of what was coming next, whatever it might be.

"I...can't right now. I'm late for an appointment." Nick did have an appointment later that day, but he was by no means late. He just lacked the skill and fortitude to handle conflict. Betty often said he only possessed the latter half of the fight-or-flee instinct.

"It's important." Her words sounded like a plea.

"I have to go...but I want to talk to you, too. I have something important to discuss as well. Can it wait until tonight, though?" Nick set the paper down and picked up his briefcase on the way to the door.

"But ... you didn't even eat your breakfast."

"I'm not very hungry," he said. "Besides, there's a hair in it. Actually, there's a few. It just took away my appetite." Nick knew it was an unbelievable and transparently snobbish thing to say, but he couldn't think of anything else. As he opened the front door, he added, "I'll see you tonight. We'll talk then." There was no response, not even the standard sigh that he expected.

The handle jiggled as he opened the front door, as if it could only take a few more turns before falling apart. It was old like the house and had survived about as long as anyone could have expected. Nick looked it over for a short moment before casually turning toward his car. *'I'll have to fix that.'*

When walking to the vehicle, a ten-year-old four-door sedan he was thinking of trading in for something more current, Nick noticed that he couldn't see the mailbox at the end of the driveway. Wondering what was amiss, he trudged through the snow to inspect the damage. Apparently, use and old age had caused the box to dislodge from its wooden base. It now formed a cylindrical lump in the snow where it had fallen. Nick's attitude was much the same as with the door-knob and he simply leaned over, picked up the metal box, brushed it off, and set it back in its place. *'Nothing a hammer and nails can't fix.'*

He then walked to his car, opened the driver's side door, knocked the snow from his new shoes, got in, and started the engine, which started at the third attempt. The dashboard sparked to life, and in red block letters, strategically placed where they could not be missed, the message 'CHANGE OIL SOON' added yet another chore to Nick's 'to-do' list. *'I guess there's a lot of stuff around here that needs to be fixed'*, he thought as he drove away under the impression that his front door, his mailbox, his car, his marriage, and his life were all in a similar state of disrepair.

At 7am the streets are typically vacant, and Nick would have made good time on his way to campus, if campus were his destination. He managed to get within a few blocks of his office before turning away into a section of rented housing used mostly by the graduate student population. While campus housing left a lot to be desired by his standards, at least most of the yards were devoid of the party remnants and empty beer kegs so common in the neighbouring streets. Nick sloshed into a large, asphalt, unploughed car park and parked in the only available spot, in about half-a-foot of icy slush. He made fresh footprints in the new snow while ascending a set of exterior wooden stairs to the third floor and then knocked on the aluminium door to apartment 3C. While waiting for the door to open, Nick looked to his right and left, then behind him to see if his arrival had been witnessed by any of the neighbours. Knowing the nature of the average college student, even the average graduate student, he felt assured that the likelihood of anyone being awake at this time of the morning was not something he should get overly worried about.

Nick heard the metallic slide of a chain lock, the quick turn of a deadbolt, and then the door opened. Maggie Malone, the auburn haired third-year doctoral student, stood in the opening wearing a smile and the pink satin robe Nick had bought for her the week before. She didn't wear the short robe as much as she held it up off the ground with her shoulders. The slightest of breezes could have sent it sliding down Maggie's endless legs to collect in a gentle pile at her feet, leaving her dressed in only the smile. It was tied carelessly around her waist and the V-shaped folds hung dangerously loose about her breasts.

Nick tried to speak, but could not. Instead he just stood in the doorway, mouth agape like a stunned boy seeing his first *Playboy* magazine after stealing it from his father's collection. Nick studied her, taking in all the minor intricacies that make women so wonderfully unique and similar at the same time. A waterfall of ginger curls fell down over her shoulders as she tilted her shy head forward and tried not to look back. Nick watched as the young woman he had been sleeping with for the past six months chewed on her bottom lip in nervous anticipation, unaware of just how much time had passed. Feeling like a stunned child, Nick put his right hand to his chin and forced his paralysed mouth closed. Maggie let out a playful giggle at this and did the speaking for him.

"I made breakfast," she said. "You hungry?"

"S-Starving."

Sex, the vigorous and playfully naughty kind that had been so vacant from Nick's life in recent years, filled the next hour-and-a-half of the morning. This had become the morning routine of late, one that Nick was getting used to. Once the act was complete and the guilt washed away in a cheap apartment shower, Nick and Maggie settled down at the kitchen table for a cup of coffee to discuss their plans, his lesson plans for the day, and their combined plan to run away together.

"What's the lecture about today, Nick? Still teaching that Dickens text?"

"Yep. Today we're going to explore the concept of greed by examining a character named Silas Wegg." Wegg was a character from a lesser-known work, so Nick was pleasantly surprised when Maggie knew of him.

"He's the peg-legged guy, right?"

"You are correct, my dear," Nick replied as Maggie walked over to the sink to do the dishes. *'Betty would never know that, nor would she care.'* He noticed a small coffee stain on the back of Maggie's robe and couldn't help but form a nostalgic smile. In that moment, for just an instant, the poorly built, poorly furnished box apartment became a different place, a better place, and he became a different person, a younger person. The moment ended in the form of a single word question followed by a bombshell.

"Nick?" Maggie asked. "Did you tell her yet?"

"No." Before he could go on, Maggie interrupted him. She stood with her back to the sink, leaning against it with her palms on the countertop. Her naked feet side-by-side, her legs and back formed a straight line up to her delicate neck, and then to her angry face. Nick studied her features, the smallish nose, her subtle cheekbones, the tiny freckles that dotted her face and chest so lightly that only those allowed into her personal space knew they were there. Her lips, which curled up slightly when she smiled, also did so when she frowned. Even when her face wore the furrowed brow and glare, Nick found her absolutely beautiful.

"You promised," she said. "You promised me you would tell her. It's been six months. For six months you've been telling me you were going to leave her."

"I know, Maggie. I'm going to tell her tonight and I'll be out by the weekend. Everything is in order. I have a place all lined up, for both of us." Nick watched as the scared face of his mistress washed away like a sandcastle in the tide, gone in a single giant wave and replaced by that same playful smile, and a look of almost childlike anticipation.

"I love you, Nick."

Nick smiled and grabbed her by the waist, pulling her down to his lap. He kissed her several times before becoming aware of the time. "I have to go," he said, "I have a meeting with Dr. Ellington in ten minutes."

"What's it about?" Maggie asked.

"Don't know. It happened last second – I only found out yesterday. Probably just some procedural nonsense." With that, Nick stood to leave.

"Want to take your coffee with you?" she asked, cheerfully playing the role of the next housewife.

"No thanks," he said, "I don't really like that brand." With a quick smile, Nick turned and left, closing the door a little too hard on the way out, rattling the cheap Michelangelo prints on the outside wall.

Nick got back in his car and turned the key in the ignition, and again the car struggled against him before eventually agreeing to take him where he needed to go. The roads, however, were not so easily subdued. The snow had begun to fall again about an hour earlier, and the whole world seemed coated in a fresh layer of the fluffy white annoyance. The snow hadn't been shovelled away since the night before and with the new inch or so that had fallen in the past hour, things were getting pretty messy on the roads.

When Nick put the car in reverse, it didn't move. The tires just spun and spun, digging deeper, looking for a firm hold, but finding none. Like a fish in a fisherman's net, the car entangled itself deeper with every effort to escape. And so did its driver, with every press of the accelerator. *'Dammit. I should have signed that stupid petition'*, he thought as he remembered a group of students who visited him a month or so earlier. They asked him to sign a petition asking the university to get involved in housing matters concerning its students. That way, the local landlords couldn't tell students to go screw themselves when housing situations presented themselves – like snow removal. It was a nice thought, but Nick believed that the university would look disapprovingly on any faculty member who signed, so he refused, wishing the students luck instead. The petition flopped, and now, in some strange display of meteorological karma, he had to pay the price.

While thinking about what to do next, Nick's mind wandered back to the last time he got himself stuck in the snow. It happened a few years before in the stone driveway of his home, back when his old car was new. Snow had piled up to near blizzard heights, but Betty wanted a bottle of wine and Nick was determined to get her one. The attempt at belated chivalry, one that Betty tried unsuccessfully to refuse, was an attempt to rekindle an already fluttering spark. Nick made it about six or seven feet from where he had started before the predictable occurred and he could go no further. After a couple of minutes spent watching her silly Prince Charming try to dig himself out, Betty came out of the house with hot coffee. The couple laughed and joked, threw snowballs at each other and made angels in the front yard, one slightly taller than the other. They built an artificial person in the snow and then went inside and upstairs with thoughts of making their second child. Conception escaped them, but both called it an afternoon well spent. Now it felt far away, like a memory that would soon disappear altogether, like those we let go of when one stage of life begins and another ends – as a child forgets their first trip to Disney because they're simply too young to hang onto the memory.

Nick stepped out of the car to inspect the size and scope of the obstacle, taking with him the plastic scraper the dealer gave him ten years before. Up and down the street he saw people digging their cars out of the car parks. It made Nick rethink his attendance policy since he was usually less than forgiving on the subject of tardy students. Getting stuck in a student car park gave him a bit of perspective, forced him to see the situation from someone else's point-of-view. As he used the undersized tool to clear a path for the back tires, he silently decided to start class a few minutes later in January. He waited. He waited for someone to come outside with coffee, to throw snowballs with him and to make angels, though he knew it wouldn't happen. Maggie was beautiful, but delicate, and rarely if ever strained herself or exposed herself to anything she deemed 'unpleasant'. Nick knew the best he could expect was a sympathetic look from an upstairs window.

After ten minutes of digging, and five more manoeuvring the car back and forth like a two-ton toy, Nick finally broke through and escaped. *'Now I'm really late'*, he thought. He tried to make up a bit of time on the roads, but conditions were too slick and he was forced to limp along, adding minutes to the excuse he would have to make when he managed to arrive at Dr. Ellington's office. Luckily, Nick found an open parking space in a freshly ploughed car park just outside Anderson Hall, where the English department offices were housed. Nick moved as quickly as he could considering the slippery pavement and dashed through the front door, and into a waiting elevator.

"Third floor, please," he said to the woman standing next to the row of buttons and he prepared for the uncomfortable feeling that hit him in the belly every time he took the lift. It reminded him of riding in his father's old truck as a young boy, when his dad would drive over the crest of a hill a little too fast and the vehicle would threaten to leave the pavement, and little Nicky's bladder would threaten to release itself into his pants.

Three dings later, the elevator arrived at the third floor. Nick's wet shoes almost slipped out from under him as he rounded the corner on the beige-tiled floor and clip-clopped his way to the office at the end of the hall.

The hallway terminated in a wall of four-inch glass blocks with a heavy oak door in the centre. A design student completed the work in the seventies as part of a graduate program and, shortly after, that student became the subject of jokes among the faculty. The gaudy clouded glass, the green plastic nameplate on the door, and the beige tile with flecks of brown in it combined to make the current department feel either nostalgic or slighted by the university for their lack of concern for updating the office space. Design students now did their projects on a volunteer basis at local businesses, mainly due to the threat of a faculty protest. The thought of it always made Nick smile, even when he was late and wet from the calf down.

Nick came face-to-face with the name 'BOB ELLING-TON' in large block letters as he turned the brass doorknob to his colleague's office. Underneath his name, in only slightly smaller lettering, he read the words 'FACULTY CHAIR'. *'Probably just a procedural thing'*, he thought, but he still felt nervous being late. Nick saw himself as someone who was never late and it would have even been true to say he was a little obsessive about appointments. Betty called him 'compulsively early' due to the nervous, twitchy attitude he would develop whenever they had to be somewhere, regardless of the importance of the event. Be it a party, or a parent-teacher conference, or a dinner reservation for that matter, Nick was always on time and expected the same of everyone else around him. An hour before they needed to leave, Nick would be fully dressed and barking questions up the stairs about how many coats of makeup Betty planned to apply to her face or how many outfits she was going to try on. Now he was late, and his own abhorrence of that fact was making him fidget.

The outer office was largely empty, with a few mismatched chairs against the glass wall for visitors and a few promotional posters displayed. The only significant piece of furniture in the room was the antique oak desk against the opposite wall, where Grace Upham sat. Grace was Dr. Ellington's assistant, a woman in her forties of apparent Asian decent and, by the look of her desk, she took her job seriously. Everything seemed to sit in its proper place, the very model of organisation. Even the pencils, which were kept in a coffee mug with the words 'World's Greatest Assistant' printed in bold black letters, were sharpened to the exact same length, without a single utensil standing higher than the rest. '*And I thought I was obsessive*', Nick reflected as he took a seat across from her.

"You can go in now, Dr. Wheeler," the secretary said. "He's expecting you." Nick had met Grace once before, at an office party the year before. After a few discussions with her that never strayed from the various gossip topics floating around the faculty, he determined that she probably knew more about him than he wanted her to. Sitting behind that perfect desk, with her hair pulled up in a perfect little bun, she looked at his dishevelled appearance as if she were judging him. As he rose and passed her by, Nick decided that he didn't like obsessive people and that he would have to try to lighten up a bit himself so others would not see him as he saw Grace Upham.

"Good morning, Nick," Dr Ellington said. "Have a seat."

"Morning, Bob. Sorry I'm late."

"Don't worry about it. Make yourself comfortable."

Nick placed his briefcase next to the brown leather chair he chose to sit in and surveyed the room. While not as orderly as the outer office, the room possessed the dignified manner that the position required and that defied the architectural monstrosity it appeared to be from the outside. Bob had the same diplomas and degrees on his wall that Nick hung on his own, though the schools named on them carried with them a bit more prestige than the places where Nick studied. Though he did suffer from a bit of professional envy, Nick never bore any real resentment towards his boss. What Nick did resent, however, was the giant bookcase against the left wall of the room, which stood full of wonderful old volumes of great literary works. First editions, signed copies, and even Bob's own book – a well respected commentary on the Romantic period in England. This always made Nick feel insignificant, like he was treading water as others were swimming by. He had managed to be published in a few minor journals but, taken as a whole, his accomplishments simply didn't measure up, and the bookcase reminded him of that.

Bob Ellington sat in a high-backed leather swivel chair and, from behind a considerable stack of what appeared to be personnel files and forms, a smile crossed his round, cherubic face. *'Well, at least I'm better looking'*, Nick thought as he looked at the overweight literary giant with the bad, grey moustache and the male pattern baldness. Bob leaned forward, put his palms on the oak desk, and started the meeting.

"Nick, we've known each other for quite a few years now, right?"

"Seven, if memory serves," Nick added.

"That sounds about right. During that time, I'd like to think we've become friends, at least in a professional sense, right?"

'What does that mean: "in a professional sense"? What's he getting at?' After a short pause, Nick responded. "Sure, I guess you could say that."

"I do say that, and I say it because the question I am about to ask is going to sound like I'm prying into your personal life and I want you to know that I only ask with the best of intentions." By this point, Nick found himself a bit confused. He thought the meeting would be concerned with what classes he would be teaching in the upcoming term, or about the results of the teacher evaluations his students filled out the week before, or some other matter of small importance. Bob had never asked about his personal life before, and something about his asking now felt strange, like he was being forced to do it.

"The question I want to ask," Dr. Ellington continued, "is in reference to your wife, Betty." Bob looked uncomfortable and shifted slightly in his chair before going on. "Is...everything all right at home, Nick?"

A slap in the face wouldn't have struck him with the same dizzying force as that question. There appeared to be no reason for it, at least until Nick gave it a second to sink in. *'He knows.'*

Instantly, Nick began forming scenarios in his head – a student seeing him go into Maggie's apartment, telling another, a rumour starts, that rumour inevitably finds its way to Grace Upham's waiting clutches before being placed, in all its glory, on Bob Ellington's desk. Nick sat up straight and tried to hide the panic welling up inside. Faculty members, especially married ones, were supposed to keep a safe distance from the student body. Sex with a student was a crime so abhorred by the university that is was referred to as 'the eighth deadly sin'. Nick's stomach churned as his career flashed before his eyes. *'This is just the beginning. There'll be a hearing.*

Everyone will know. I'll be ruined.' Despite the terror behind his eyes, Nick kept his demeanour calm and decided to play stupid. "I'm not sure I know what you're talking about, Bob."

Dr. Ellington shifted in his chair again. "Well, normally I wouldn't say anything, but Sharon asked me to speak to you. Well, actually, she forced me to." *'I knew it.'* Sharon Ellington, despite her bossy nature, was generally thought of as a kind and caring woman. She and Betty played cards together once a month or so, part of what they jokingly called the 'Career Widow's Club,' and the two considered themselves friends. Bob sat up straight and began telling the rest of the story.

"Well, as you know, Nick, my wife runs that little antique shop across from the church." *'Where's he going with this?'* "Well, with those big windows in front of the store, Sharon sees quite a bit of what goes on around town, and some things she has seen lately have worried her a little."

Nick wracked his brain, trying to think of times he and Maggie might have been in front of that store, but couldn't think of any. They hadn't been there. They had been careful.

"What's she worried about, Bob?" Nick asked, feigning mystification.

"Well," *'I swear, every sentence this man speaks starts with that word'*, "Sharon has seen Betty at the church across the street quite a bit in the last couple of weeks."

"Well," Nick said, "That's not necessarily odd. Betty likes to attend services." Nick no longer feigned confusion. He was truly perplexed.

"There's more, Nick. The minister often stops in the shop during his lunch hour, so Sharon naturally asked about Betty. You know, to see how she was doing." *'Looking for gossip, no doubt.'* "The minister said she has just been sitting there, day in, day out, for the last two weeks, refusing to speak to anyone."

Nick didn't know what to say, but he couldn't help feeling some small kind of relief that the conversation appeared to be going in a different direction. Perhaps he had managed to avoid the crucifixion he felt sure was coming just a few moments before. After the initial selfish thoughts of his self-protection subsided, the confusion returned. *What is she doing? She's always been more inclined to go to the church than me, but two weeks non-stop?* As he replayed the tale in his head, and threw in what he knew about his own indiscretions, the answer came to him. *She knows. Betty knows.*

"Nick," Bob continued, "Sharon and I want to let you know that if there's anything we can do...well...if there is any way we can help..." Nick looked up at Bob Ellington and felt ashamed of himself. He couldn't place where the feeling came from, but he somehow knew he did not deserve the offered kindness.

"I understand, Bob. And thanks. I wasn't aware. I'll go and speak to her after work and see what I can do."

"Take the day off, Nick."

The words had come out in a commanding tone Nick did not recognise. He looked up to see a serious look on Bob's face and likened it to a father scolding a child.

"What?"

"Nick, whatever's troubling Betty, I think you should take care of it sooner rather than later. Go on over to the church and speak to your wife." Nick had never heard Bob speak this way before and, despite his need to defy authority, he stood up and collected his things. Then, as if by instinct, Nick reached over the desk holding out his right hand, which Bob accepted and shook.

"Thanks, Bob."

"Don't mention it."

Nick left the office and, without any awareness of the passing of time, he found himself in his car driving towards the section of town where Betty's church stood. As he turned onto the street, Nick realised he hadn't the first clue what he would say to his wife when he saw her. *'What am I going to say? How am I going to say it? How does a man go about telling his wife that he's leaving her?'*

Then a very different thought came to him, another difficulty he had not yet considered. *'I can't tell her in a church.'* Nick turned his head to the right and looked out the passenger side window to see the statue of Mary outside the First Assembly Church of God, the place where Betty had been spending so much of her time of late. Standing tall and perfect, arms outstretched in an inviting grace, Mary seemed to be telling him that everything would be all right in the end. Nick kept driving, strangely satisfied at the notion that he had apparently found a line of hypocrisy he was incapable of crossing. While the sin of adultery did not deter him, the idea of bringing that sin with him into the church seemed enough to keep the car moving. *'I guess it's a start.'*

When Nick pulled into the driveway, the rusted mailbox lay in the yard again, covered in a new layer of snow. Again he trudged through the small front yard to retrieve it. Nick brushed it off with the sleeve of his coat and placed it back on its perch. The moment he removed his hand, though, the box toppled and fell once again. *'That's it. I'm going to fix this thing once and for all. Besides, I have some time to kill.'* So, with his mind sufficiently distracted, Nick walked towards the house on his way to the basement, where he kept what tools he had acquired over the years. The front doorknob came off in his hand, giving him another task to pass the time. He replaced the handle and closed the door behind him.

As Nick entered the house, the imperfections of the place

smothered him like an attacking swarm of wasps. The subtle nicks and scrapes that any lived-in place endures as years pass by now seemed large and grotesque. A scratch in the coffee table became the size of a canyon, the small stain on the carpet in the corner of the room now dominated the entire floor. Lamps were cracked, furniture torn, paint chipped in every room of the house. Nick had just never noticed it before. What opened his eyes still remained a mystery, but now that they were open, the task of repair seemed almost too large to begin.

Nick opened the door to the basement and descended the stairs on his way to the small workbench he kept in the darkest corner. After looking through his meagre collection of tools, all he could find was an old wood-handled hammer he broke years ago while trying to mend a broken fence, a task still unfinished and untended. The rotted handle had snapped and put an end to a job Nick never wanted to start in the first place. Now that he wanted a hammer, though, there was nothing suitable for the job. Nick was debating the idea of a trip to the hardware shop when he heard the creak of the front door. It was only noon. He hadn't expected Betty to be home so soon. He considered the possibility of staying in the basement and never going upstairs ever again, but after a moment he understood that even he wouldn't go that far just to avoid conflict. He had to face this. He had to tell her he was leaving. He climbed the stairs slowly, but with his resolve firmly in place.

"Nick, what are you doing home so early?" she asked as he exited the basement and crept into the kitchen.

"I wanted to talk to you," he said, "and I just couldn't wait until the end of the day." He left out the part about his conversation with Bob Ellington and the fact that he had been ordered home from work.

"I'm glad you're here," she said. "I have something I need to talk to you about, too. Why don't I put on some coffee for us?" Betty's voice sounded calm and even, making Nick think of the Mary statue and what it might sound like if it could talk.

Nick sat at the table and almost picked up the paper that still lay there, but thought better of it, deciding to sit quietly and wait for Betty to join him. A few minutes later, Betty placed a mug of coffee in front of him and one in front of the seat across from him. She moved over to the other side of the table and gracefully placed herself in the chair directly opposite her husband.

Whether a product of her time in the church or from his knowledge of that time, Nick couldn't help but detect a change in her appearance. He couldn't place it, couldn't identify a feature that differed from the day before, but she looked like a different person. Her hair shone like golden silk, her blue eyes brightened somehow, and she almost appeared to glow.

Betty sat with her back straight and looked at him from behind her coffee, without an ounce of worry or anger on her face. Expecting the crying and despair that any soon-to-be-jilted wife would be expected to display, he found himself dumbfounded by the angelic calm he saw in front of him. Nick, though, was resolved to do what he had put off for so long, so he raised his mug to take a sip and spoke.

"There's something I need to tell you."

"Me too," she interrupted, "but I'm afraid I must go first." Frustration flooded his face. To face the problem was one thing, but to do it when she said so was quite another. *'I have to get this out'*, he thought, and then added to himself: *'I have to get out of this house'*. Betty picked up on the change in his features, but calmly went on. "I'm sorry Nick, but you will understand in just a minute."

"Okay, Betty. Go ahead," he said, trying to keep himself a little more calm and a little less transparent. Nick took another sip of his coffee and, just as the cup hit his lip, he noticed something odd. There was something in his coffee, floating on the surface. Betty paused.

Nick set the mug down on the table and removed the foreign object. He held it up in front of him, letting the light of the room wash over it. It belonged to Betty, was a part of her, actually. The item floating in his coffee turned out to be a single strand of her golden hair. He finally understood. Like the last crucial piece of a giant jigsaw puzzle, all the clues fitted together to form a complete picture. Nick's gaze fell on his wife's face and, before he could get the question out of his mouth, Betty Wheeler, his wife of seventeen years, confirmed his fears with three simple words.

"I have cancer."

Surprise collided with disbelief and the world stood on its head. All the noises of the room – the ticking clock, the percolations of the coffee-maker, the tapping of a nervous adulterer's fingernails on the table – went silent, leaving Nick alone with only the sound of his thumping heart to keep him company. Everything in his field of vision turned a shade of yellow, and Nick suddenly felt like he was falling. He no longer smelled or tasted the coffee he had not yet swallowed. His senses were failing him, with the exception of one. His sense of touch. He could still feel. Something, someone touched him on the hand and order began to fight the chaos and despair. Slowly, Nick's vision cleared, his hearing returned, and he straightened himself in his chair. When he returned from his fit of senselessness and regained his composure, Betty was still there, gently holding his hand. Her expression remained unchanged. She sat serenely, waiting for him to take in the news and to produce the question she knew would be his first.

"Is it…?" He couldn't say the word.

"Terminal?" She said it for him. "Yes, it's terminal. I'm afraid it will happen soon."

"How long have you known?" Nick asked.

"Four weeks. I started the chemotherapy ten days ago."

"Why didn't you...why didn't you tell me?" Nick, in all his selfishness, felt somehow betrayed. He felt like he deserved to know and that she had deprived him of his rightful knowledge. He was an outsider in his own home.

"Nick," she responded, "Are you sure you want an answer to that question?"

"I...," he tried, but there was no response to her question. He didn't want the answer. He already knew it. She felt, no, she knew he would leave her. After seventeen years of quiet desperation, his wife knew him well. He would run. He wanted to run. Nick's eyes darted about the room, and again the swarm of imperfections renewed their attack. The room felt small and the air close. The urge to flee won the struggle within him, and Nick could hold it off no longer.

"I...I have to go." The clumsy sentence fell out of his mouth as he stood. Nick expected a desperate response, something to shame him into staying in his chair. None came. Instead, Betty sat calmly, as if his actions were no surprise to her at all. Nick didn't stop to ponder this. He went for the door as fast as he could manage.

Again, time passed without his knowledge, and again he found himself behind the wheel of his car. But this time he drove without any real objective. He looked out of the window at the trees and their empty limbs, thinking about his morning daydream and his desire for a new life. The high limbs were no longer dancing, no longer raising their prayers to Heaven. They were pointing at him, like numerous accusing fingers in the air. Everywhere he looked, whether in front, behind or to either side, the fingers were there. Nick drove towards town, hoping it would be a place more sympathetic and with fewer trees.

As he reached the outskirts of the neighbouring village, he found himself scanning the streets, looking for a place familiar to him, some place he could think of as friendly. Continuing on, he ventured closer to campus and his anxiety lessened, if only by a small amount. Nick pulled up along the side of the road and parked outside a rare bookstore, one of his favourite haunts. He gathered himself after a few moments and stepped out of the car, thinking the sight and dusty smell of the literature inside would help him think, help him make sense of things. But as he approached the front door, he saw something he did not expect.

Maggie.

Before he could turn away, she saw him in the window and walked out to speak with him. Wearing tight brown pants and a tighter beige blouse under her jacket, Maggie looked perfectly costumed for her role as a home-wrecker. "I heard your classes were cancelled today," she said.

"Word travels fast."

"Relax, Nick. I'm not spying on you or anything. My friend Angie told me. She's in your morning class." Maggie spoke so matter-of-factly and the sound of it felt like an insult, like she had no heart. Nick knew this was a silly thought, since she couldn't possibly know what had happened, but he was angry with her just the same. Nick looked around at the other shops – a trendy coffee shop, a small Jewish deli, and a hardware store across the street – to see if his open air discussion with his mistress was being scrutinised by anyone he knew. As he surveyed their surroundings, Maggie asked him another question.

"So, did you go home?"

"Just ask me what you want to ask me," Nick snapped, wanting to cut through all the hedging.

"Okay, fine." she snapped right back. "Did you tell her or not?"

"I didn't tell her." Maggie placed a hand on her hip and shifted slightly to one side, a stance that all men recognise but only women can execute.

"When are you going to tell her, Nick?" Her voice mixed insistent with angry, topped with a dash of fear.

Nick looked into her eyes and played the question back in his head. He didn't have an answer. After everything he had been through, and put others through, he was still running from that question. That's where the shame was coming from. That's why he couldn't bear to be in the same room as his wife. In that instant, Nick finally understood that he was the cause of his own troubles, that nothing was simply happening to him, but all things, save his wife's disease, were his fault. Nick looked into Maggie's eyes again and decided that it was time to stop running.

"Well, Nick, when are you going to tell your wife that you're having an affair and that you're leaving her?"

"I don't know, Maggie. I just don't know, but I'm sure the time will come when I can tell her." Maggie's face began to flush.

"And what the hell is that supposed to mean?"

"It means...that I don't think we should see each other any-more." Maggie's mouth fell open and her bottom lip started to quiver. She looked as if she might explode out of her stance and strangle him, but Nick stood his ground.

"I'm sorry, Maggie, but I have to go. I have some things to fix at home." Nick turned and walked away, but he didn't go to his car. Instead, he started across the street on foot. Maggie, in a state more angry than upset, called after him.

"Where the hell are you going?" she asked.

Nick stopped in the middle of the road and turned around. With the thumb of his right hand, he pointed over his shoulder to the hardware shop across the street.

"I need to buy a new hammer."

Monday

By
Sarah James

Monday

It's a winter morning much like every other as twenty-seven-year-old Catherine Phillips climbs the twenty-nine steps up to the cold and busy platform at Lichfield City station. Many of the commuters already there still look half-asleep. She knows how that feels. She has been taking the train to her bank job in Birmingham every workday now for the past six years.

She glances at her watch, hidden under the edge of her soft leather glove. It is 7.55am, only three minutes to go. She rocks backwards and forwards on the spot in the hope it will keep her warm. But it does little to help. The mist from her breath hangs suspended in the cold air like fairy dust, but without any magical powers that could change the weather, or fly her off to a different, more exciting world.

Around Catherine, her fellow passengers are also trying to keep warm. A middle-aged woman grips a polystyrene cup of coffee tightly in her hands. A young man with a red rucksack rubs his hands together and then attempts to blow life into them with his warm breath. A man in a dark grey suit puts his briefcase down beside him on the platform and sticks his hands and mobile phone into his overcoat pockets.

Catherine doesn't know these strangers, but she has long come to recognise their faces. The same people at the same time on the same platform day after day, week after week, year after year. Each one looks expectantly for the train as if waiting for something truly momentous to happen.

At last, she hears the wheeze of the approaching engine. As the train draws near, she notices how the grey sky wraps around it like a thick woollen blanket, muffling sound and sensations. None of the other passengers seem to notice. Everyone is shuffling forward in their rush to make sure they get a seat. But she hangs back, watching from a distance for a few seconds before joining the crowd, eagerly clamouring to get onto the train. There is no pushing or shoving of elbows, but she can hear hopes and thoughts jostling each other in the race to board the carriage.

Lichfield City 07.58

Inside, there is little room to manoeuvre.

"Sorry," Catherine apologises as her handbag knocks a young man's arm. She hasn't noticed him on the platform or on this train before.

"That's all right," he says, looking at her, as he sits down opposite, and for the first time that day she sees colour. His eyes are brown, green and black all rolled into one.

Scared by a feeling she doesn't recognise, she forces her eyes away from his and sits down, placing her bag by her side. She looks round the carriage and finds that the earlier black and white silent movie of a cold winter morning has now become a vibrant colour film in 3D. Even the grey seats are splashed with specks of blue and green; the ashen-faced passengers have red wind-glazed cheeks and their scattered collection of hats, scarves and gloves is like a bright assortment of children's sweets.

The train is beginning to gear up for departure and, as she sits back in her seat, it feels as if the vibrations are kick-starting her body into motion. She can see everything, smell everything, feel everything.

Outside, the metal pylons have been keeping pace with the train's motion. But now the anorexic giants stretch out their long legs, striding steadfastly over the track and away across the fields on the other side of the train.

Catherine lowers her head over that day's edition of *The Metro*, so her long black hair forms a curtain in front of her eyes. She then glances up through the camouflaged hide at the young stranger opposite.

He, too, is reading the paper, his eyes moving intently

along the print. The pages rustle as he turns them. She notices a name badge pinned to the right lapel of his navy suit. 'Ben Harrington'. She looks at his face. She guesses he must be about thirty. His dark brown hair is combed firmly off his forehead. He is not strikingly good-looking, but attractive, enveloped by a scent that she cannot identify, but which seems somehow familiar. Their knees are so close they are almost touching.

Shenstone 08.02

"Tickets, please." The conductor whisks Catherine's pass away and returns it immediately. Like a conjurer, he seems to do it all without moving his hand or even looking at it. She turns to stare again at her stranger.

The conductor steps away, continuing down the centre of the carriage, where the floor has been turned into what looks like a nursery school painting by scores of commuters' wet feet.

Catherine continues staring at her stranger. Suddenly he looks up and their eyes meet. Embarrassed, she looks away at the sodden field outside. She can see a tree reflected upside down in the silver water. She feels like that tree, her world upside down.

There is something beeping. She looks back at her stranger. He pulls out his mobile phone from his hip pocket. He presses a button and the beeping stops. She wills him to look up again, away from his phone, at her.

She stares into his eyes. They are not close enough to touch, but near enough to read.

"Hello, my name's Catherine." Her eyes talk without her asking them to.

"I'm Ben," his eyes reply without hesitation. "I saw you looking at me."

"Did you?"

"But you didn't see me looking at you, did you?" his eyes tease her.

"Why were you looking at me?" her eyes ask boldly.

"I think you know why!"

She looks at him silently, the light in his eyes dances to some exotic tune as it sucks her gently inwards towards their centre.

Blake Street 08:05

The train picks up speed quickly as it pulls out of the station and the light whirls faster and faster, round and round in his eyes. They shoot through a short tunnel and the brief darkness is exhilarating. She feels giddy, intoxicated, every sensation exaggerated as his eyes move in closer and closer until they are touching her own.

The first embrace of their eyes is like the desperate gasp of a diver coming up for air, never sure when they will next get the chance to drink more oxygen. Then gradually their breathing slows and their eyes mould into a gentler embrace.

Butlers Lane 08.07

After a while their eyes separate again, and Catherine becomes aware once more of the world outside. Hedges and houses follow one after another, and then the train enters a cutting lined with trees. Some stand tall and still like elegant stick models posing for pictures at the end of a catwalk. Others are frozen in mid-pirouette with their branches flung out around them like a ballerina's hair and tutu. The thicker ones, too, have been caught in mid-step, like giant ogres preparing to crush people underfoot. All of them are staring right into her life.

She moves uneasily. Behind the mechanical whirr of the train's monotonous motion, she can hear the wind whispering, the trees talking.

"Look at them – what on earth does he see in her?"

"Mark my words, it won't last. It won't work out, I'm telling you."

Frightened by this interference, she looks over to Ben's eyes for reassurance. But they gaze at her unseeingly. The train has entered a tunnel, and all around her is dark and silent.

Four Oaks 08:10

The light returns again as they enter the station and her eyes find his again. He looks sheepish as if he knows she wants more from him than he currently feels able to give. She sees this, but is unable to stop the rebukes that flow from her eyes.

"Where were you? I needed you. You let me down."

His eyes don't respond and her's fall silent. They know this is an argument they cannot win.

Eventually the carriage slinks into another tunnel. Time and the train drag their feet as they push onwards, deeper and deeper into the darkness.

Sutton Coldfield 08:13

More people get on the train and, as the carriage fills up, Catherine smells stale sweat, the lingering scent of a fried bacon sandwich, cigarette smoke clinging desperately to a favourite coat.

"Excuse me." A pretty, blonde woman smiles as she pushes between them to sit down next to Catherine.

Catherine is about to smile back when she notices Ben looking at the woman.

"What are you staring at?" Catherine's eyes demand.

"I'm only being friendly," Ben's laugh. "You know I only have eyes for you!"

He tries to stare his way into her eyes, but the conductor moves between them to check the blonde woman's ticket.

The conductor leaves and Catherine returns her gaze to

Ben. He looks back at her. But her eyes have frozen hard, as impassive as she can make them. He continues staring until she feels them start to melt and their usual warm mahogany colour returns.

Finally, they speak. "I know, I'm sorry."

Wylde Green 08:16

Their eyes embrace again and Catherine cannot believe how different the world feels. Suddenly, everything seems perfect. The houses that fly past outside are not the squashed matchstick boxes of suburbia but the dreams of young lovers. Even the smoke rising from the chimneys weaves a cheerful pattern in the sky as it drifts past allotments and the wide green of a playing field.

Chester Road 08:17

Catherine looks out the window eagerly as the train passes more homes, then a busy road followed by a group of children in school uniform playfully kicking a soda can along the pavement.

"That could be us," her eyes suggest. "Our home, our children."

She waits for his reply, but his eyes shuffle uncomfortably away from hers as he leans forward to look out of the window. At last he turns back to her. The train is nearing Erdington.

"This is where I usually get off," his eyes stutter as he stands up.

"I see."

She slumps back in her seat. There is little else to say. She has heard this sort of thing before.

She waits for him to move, but he doesn't. His face is blank.

Erdington 08:19

The doors open. Some people get off and many more get on. The train starts moving again.

He is still there.

Catherine is quiet, her breath moving in and out to the rhythm of the train as it picks up speed.

"I'm glad you stayed," her eyes whisper finally and then they are embracing again harder and more passionately than before.

Gravelly Hill 08:21

His eyes break away as the train leaves the station and he puts his hand into his right trouser pocket. She can hear some loose change rattling as he pulls out his cotton handkerchief. He blows his nose loudly. She wishes he could be quieter, maybe use a tissue instead.

As she examines him more closely, Catherine notices his appearance is not as neat as she first thought. There is a small spot of black ink on his shirt and his tie is no longer hanging straight. To her eyes, now nothing is quite right.

"Why do you have to dress so sloppily and make such a noise blowing your nose?" her eyes reproach him.

"I'll blow my nose how I want!" his eyes reply angrily. "And what's wrong with what I'm wearing? Least I don't spend hours in front of the mirror."

"No, clearly not!" Her eyes speak more bitterly than she means them to. "Just because I try to look nice for you. I don't know why I bother!"

"I don't either. Obviously, I'm not good enough for you!"

He folds his arms and looks away from her. She turns away, too.

Aston 08:25

It is several minutes before Catherine finally looks across at him again.

"I'm sorry," her eyes say. "I didn't mean it."

"No, I'm sorry."

Their eyes embrace long and gently, their bodies bending

together as if trying to melt into one another through their fused pupils.

Duddeston 08.28

Catherine relaxes back in her seat contentedly, watching Ben's body gently bob along to the train's motion. She wonders if all couples are as sure of making it so far together as she now is that they will survive this journey. The atmosphere between them is relaxed and easy, as if they have always been together. Always is a long time, she thinks joyfully, and yet…

Somewhere deep inside of her, beyond the comfortable cocoon of familiarity, something whispers: "Is that enough? Is this really what I've been looking for? Is there nothing more to life?"

The train enters another tunnel as the conductor announces that Birmingham New Street will be the next station stop. In the darkness, Catherine looks for her reflection in the window, but cannot find herself, only a blank woman's face staring back at her and a man's face close to it. The couple look exactly like them, and yet it is not them. She wonders what their story is. Are they happy together? Have they found all the answers? Do they feel that anything is missing?

She looks towards Ben, but he has already stood up and is moving away from her as the train pulls into the station.

Birmingham New Street 08:31

Catherine follows him down the carriage.

The train has stopped, and they are at the door when he turns to look at her. He is smiling. Their eyes meet, but as she gazes into his, all she can see is her own image reflected back. There is no recognition in his eyes, no eternal link beyond the grave. He is just another stranger who has walked through her life.

The doors open and she watches as he steps off the train

and merges into the crush of commuters, leaving her to get off alone.

****

Lichfield City 07.58

Ben Harrington has just passed the first four seats in his carriage when a young woman jabs him with her handbag.

"Sorry," she murmurs, looking apologetically up at him as she sits down in the seat he was heading for.

"That's all right," he mutters good-naturedly and sits down opposite, wishing he was on his usual train instead of having to miss breakfast and squash himself onto this earlier one.

He reaches into his jacket pocket for his mobile phone. It is one of the latest models. Ben pushes the top right-hand button. The screen illuminates itself with an irritatingly cheerful jingle. He looks at it. No new messages. He sighs. This means the staff training is still on. Not his ideal working day, but essential, his boss Barry says, if he is ever to rise above deputy manager of the company's small Erdington outlet. He thinks about what Barry said when he told him he was sending him on the leadership course. "You've got to appear young and enthusiastic in this game – no good standing still if what you're selling is mobiles!" The phrase makes Ben smile wryly. He isn't one for clever slogans, not like his boss. But he has been after a promotion for more than a year. He is thirty-two, he needs it. No, they need it, particularly with the way Karen is talking at the moment.

Ben puts his phone in his hip pocket and opens the paper on his lap. He flicks through the headlines as he looks for the crossword. The pages rustle. He finds the black and white grid and pulls a biro out of his top jacket pocket, his fingers catching against a piece of plastic on the lapel. It's his name badge. He feels his cheeks grow warm and hopes that no one has noticed. Karen must have pinned it on for him. It is one of the things he loves about being married to her – an embarrassing but small and thoughtful gesture reminding him that she cares.

He stares down at the crossword and starts to read the clues. But the words blur. His mind is too bleary to focus properly. Instead, he doodles pound signs and crosses on the crinkle-edged margins. Money is everything, he thinks. The only way he can give Karen what she wants. What he wants, too, if not in the same way as her.

But Ben has done the figures, again and again and again. Each time the answer is the same. They can't afford a baby. Not even if she keeps on working at the hairdressers. They barely live a comfortable life as it is. A baby would be like a permanent direct debit of several hundred pounds a month. Cash they haven't got – whatever Karen says.

Shenstone 08.02

He wishes he could make her understand. It hurts every time she brings up the subject and he has to face that pleading look in her eyes. It isn't that he doesn't want children. He would love kids. Preferably a son, not that he would admit that to Karen – a son to play with and to kick the football around in the garden. But then a daughter would be good too – a daughter who would look up at him with big adoring eyes as he read her bedtime story.

But what sort of a life could he give them?

Ben looks up. The woman opposite is smiling at him, but he isn't in the mood for early morning commuter pleasantries. He looks down again.

"Ticket please, sir."

Ben hands his ticket to the conductor, who glances at it, marks it with his blue biro and passes it quickly back. Ben wonders if the man enjoys his work, if there's much training, leadership courses, the need to impress and all that kind of thing. The job certainly looks easier than what he has to do, just walking down a train and ringing a few tickets, no having to hard sell to customers who know best and don't listen to word he says. Ben sighs. The pay's probably better too.

It's all very well for Karen to say that money doesn't matter, that they could make some savings here, cut a few corners there, that he could look for a better job or work harder for promotion. If only it was that easy. She makes it sound so simple, as black and white as his crossword grid. But the reality is as cryptic as the clues.

Ben hears his mobile phone beeping and pulls it out of his hip pocket. Damn! Low battery. He switches the phone off to stop the noise. He'll have to try and borrow a charger from someone on the course. There isn't even enough power now to turn it back on again, let alone text Karen when he finds out what time the training will finish.

He sits there, staring at his blank mobile phone screen.

Blake Street 08.05
"Ticket please, sir," the conductor asks for a second time.

Ben pulls his ticket out, wondering whether to tell the man that he has already checked it. But the conductor is looking flustered now and it's not like Ben has anything better to do during the monotony of the journey.

The conductor stares at the ticket for a while, squiggles on it for a second time and then hands it back. Ben returns to gazing at his switched-off mobile phone.

He is still staring at it when there is a beep announcing a new text. He reads it quickly.

'Congrats! U've got the job!'

Ben smiles, his whole face dancing with delight. It is what he has been waiting for. Promotion at last. Barry is moving back to Derby, as he's always talked about doing, and he, Ben, is now the new manager of the Erdington store – the boss, the one in charge, the one with the biggest pay packet.

He imagines telling Karen. She will be so pleased. They'll have to get a takeaway to celebrate and he can get in some lagers. For him, of course – no alcohol for her, not now she's pregnant.

Butlers Lane 08.07

Ben is still smiling as the train stops.

Sales are on the up. In fact, they are "better than ever before" according to Neil, the area manager. The staff are all happy, sickness is down, he has been nominated for a company award and he is waiting to hear from Neil about the manager's position at the Birmingham city centre store.

They only interviewed the last candidate yesterday afternoon, but Neil has assured him this is a formality.

"No one could beat your figures, mate," he said, with a wink. "They don't stand a chance."

But the waiting is still agonising – stomach wrenching and adrenaline bursting at the same time. Ben looks at the mobile phone on his knee. He wishes it would ring.

Four Oaks 08.10

Beep! He closes his eyes and breathes in deeply before reading his text from Neil.

'Told u m8! Start at Brum 1 dec. Drinx r on u!'

He breathes out again, his mind swirling as endorphins fizz through his arteries like champagne bubbles.

"Ben Harrington, you've come a long way. I always knew you'd turn out well, son." He can feel his body swell as he imagines his mum and dad's pride. This job is IT. More responsibility, more respect, better bonuses and a larger salary than he ever dreamed of – nearly twice what he's on now.

He tries to slow his excited breathing and think calmly about what this will mean.

They'll be able to think about buying their own place, or at least renting somewhere bigger. Karen can give up her hairdressers' job to look after their son, Matthew, and the new baby she is expecting in six weeks' time. In fact, he might suggest she stop straight away and take it easy for the rest of the pregnancy. She's always moaning about how heavy her feet feel and how much they ache. There'll be extra money for Christmas presents and they could go away on a family holiday next summer. He can't wait to tell her. Things couldn't get any better.

Sutton Coldfield 08.13

"Excuse me." A young, blonde woman smiles as she pushes past Ben to sit down on a nearby seat.

He smiles back, relaxing in the warmth of her friendliness, and continues smiling as he watches the conductor check her ticket.

Her smile reminds him of Karen's, big-mouthed and toothy, a real smile. Not that he sees much of it these days. She is usually too tired by the time he gets home. He doesn't even get back in time to give his son a kiss. He is spending more and more time at work and it's starting to get to him. It isn't just the long hours, it's the people as well – and the continuous bickering and back-stabbing driven by ambition.

Paranoia starts to bite at the back of Ben's brain. He looks out of the side of his eyes at the blonde woman. Why is she smiling at him? Is she one of them? One of those new assertive, young women he has been warned about, the ones who are after their male colleagues' jobs? Is she trying to elbow him out of the way like the others he works with, using her good looks to wheedle her way to promotion?

Now that he is looking it seems to Ben that the young

woman opposite has also been watching him. Her makeup-caked face staring at him so intently it's aggressive. She must be one of them too. How many are there?

He scowls. Things have not been the same since he left Erdington. The atmosphere at the city store is less friendly. Everyone is in a rush, everyone has something to say, everything is sales and figures and getting one over everyone else. He still can't believe someone on his own staff ruined his award chances by laying a false complaint. Him fudging the Christmas sales figures – it was ridiculous. But by the time it was sorted out, it was too late.

Wylde Green 08.16

'When will u b home?' Ben's phone beeps.

He is about to reply to Karen's text when a fat man, who is trying to squeeze his way down the train, knocks him in the stomach with a briefcase.

"Watch it," Ben snarls, his eyes narrowing.

The man stumbles an apology.

But Ben turns away. He has heard it before from others jostling for his position – niceties and then a nasty stab in the back. He won't be fooled.

He turns to his phone and taps quickly: 'Dunno. c u when i c u.' He hits the send button sharply and, without waiting to see if there's a reply, he turns to scour the latest sales figures. These are more important than ever, now that Neil is in disgrace after his affair led to accusations of harassment. The area manager's job is up for grabs and Ben is determined to get it. He has been working on the promotion for weeks, putting in long hours at the store and taking the company directors out for drinks. He sighs as he calculates that he needs to drive up sales another five per cent. This isn't going to be easy. He yawns and rubs his forehead. His face is looking wan and his eyes rarely smile anymore. Still, he's bringing home some good bonuses and, if nothing else, the area manager's job would be a welcome way out of the unfriendly Birmingham city centre store.

Chester Road 08.17

The train stops and Ben drags his head up slowly. His whole body feels heavy. It takes so much energy to move. He looks out of the window but takes nothing in. He can't concentrate on anything these days. No wonder his sales figures have taken a downturn. Having Kev, the new area manager, on the phone every day isn't helping either.

He wishes he hadn't finished his bottle of Rescue Remedy. He's not sure it does anything – it tastes too weak and watery to give much of a kick – but it's better than nothing. He'd take more Prozac, but his doctor has only prescribed two a day. Besides, he's already taking St John's Wort and, despite his surreptitious care in slipping the pills into his mouth discreetly, he has been getting side glances at work. He has the feeling people are talking about him.

The train is nearing Erdington. As it pulls past the dark, wooden station railings, Ben starts to get up. Then he remembers – this is not his stop.

Erdington 08.19

The train starts to move again. Ben stares out the window at the higgledy-piggledy houses with their peculiar odd bits jutting out from the brick. A similar mad mixture of brickwork decorates the road from the station to Erdington High Street. His eyes know the route off by heart. It is comfortingly familiar.

He looks down at his phone, resting it on his stomach at a forty-five degree angle. His belly feels empty and angry. He wishes he had time for breakfast these days. He hasn't even got any lunch to eat. Karen doesn't make him sandwiches any more. He might be able to grab a biscuit at work with his coffee, but it could be dinnertime before he has the chance to eat real food. He sighs. He doesn't know what he'll have. He's tired of Chinese, Indian and pizza. It's takeaways or nothing most nights these days as Karen is either too busy to cook or the meal she's cooked has gone cold by the time he gets home.

Ben sighs again at the thought of the long day ahead and the dark walk home afterwards from the station. It isn't even as though he gets anything from working so hard. The longer he works, the more he earns, but the more money he brings home, the more they spend. He doesn't know how they do it, but Karen says she needs new clothes and highlights in her hair so she looks like a manager's wife, and he knows she can't do without the new gym she's joined. Since Matthew has started school there is always something he needs too. Even Amy keeps coming home from nursery asking for a fairy outfit, ballerina's tutu, witch costume, and so on.

Gravelly Hill 08.21

Ben lowers his head and burrows his hand into his pocket. Loose change rattles as pulls out a crumpled handkerchief and noisily blows his nose. He shoves it back into his bulging pocket. He hasn't emptied that out for weeks. Not since Karen last made him. Not since she left.

His right hand rubs against the edge of the seat. Ouch! The ironing burn on his wrist looks angry and red against his pale skin, and his shirt cuffs are grey and grimy. He can't get the marks to come out. He can't get his ties to lie straight either. He looks from the end of his striped tie down his hand towards his blotchy fingers. The wedding ring Karen finally got him to wear after five years of marriage glints bitterly at him in the artificial train light.

Aston 08.25

'Where were u?' Karen's angry text buzzes across his

mobile screen in black tombstone lettering.

'Sorry. L8 meeting. On train. B there soon,' he texts back.

'Don't bother. Kids in bed.'

'I'll call 2 sort another time.'

'No. U'll wake them. Amy v upset. I don't want u 2 c them. U'll only let them down again.'

'Please Karen. I won't, I promise. U call me.'

Ben sits back in his seat to wait, his eyes fixed on his mobile phone screen. It remains blank.

Duddeston 08.28

'Where r u?'

Ben barely takes in the text. Instead, he stares at it blankly as if he is looking at something else, at something or nothing beyond the screen.

A minute later the phone beeps again. It is the same message but a different number.

It beeps again.

This time he doesn't even look. There's no point. Karen only wants to talk about the divorce and Kev, the area manager, only wants to see him so he can sack him.

Ben runs his dry tongue over his even drier lips. He feels all shaky. He could do with another whisky.

"Ladies and gentlemen, we are now approaching Birmingham New Street. May I remind customers…" the conductor's hissy announcement slithers its way through to the conscious part of Ben's brain, "a non-smoking station…", loosening the noose of his thoughts, "all belongings with you…" and the invisible chain tying his eyes to his mobile phone. "Birmingham New Street, this is your next station stop," the conductor concludes.

Ben stands up.

Birmingham New Street 08.31

He is already at the door when the train stops. He looks

back towards his seat for his mobile phone and then smiles as he realises he is holding it in his hand.

As he looks up, Ben notices the expression in the eyes of the woman who was sitting opposite him. She is nowhere near as pretty as Karen, but he imagines he can see in her face the light of his wife's animated eyes when she talks to him. He loves it when Karen looks at him like that.

Ben smiles at the woman, grateful for the reminder of his wife. But, of course, the woman has no idea who he is or why her eyes have made him so happy. He turns his back to her and puts his hand up to press open the doors. Then he looks down at the mobile.

The phone screen is black and blank. It is still switched-off. He must charge it straight away so he can call Karen to suggest they get fish and chips for tea. No point worrying about the money, Ben thinks, as he steps off the train quickly, leaving his fellow passengers behind, but still carrying the image of his wife's face in his mind. The odd treat won't do any harm, and they can talk again about starting a family.

****

Lichfield Trent Valley 07.55
If there's one thing train conductor Phil Bucknell hates, it's early shifts, particularly after a series of late ones. He yawns and rubs his eyes. The Lichfield to Longbridge train doesn't boast a buffet car or refreshment trolley, so he can't even sneak a quick coffee to wake himself up.

He starts his amble down the first carriage, collecting tickets unenthusiastically from the commuters who have just boarded the train. Most join at the next station, Lichfield City, where they will be arriving – he looks at his watch – in about thirty seconds.

As the train starts to slow, Phil creeps into the tiny toilet to glance in the mirror. The cabin smells of disinfectant and urine, and he notes there is water on the floor already as he holds his breath and frowns at his reflection, quickly brushing his fingers through his curly, pine hair. Then he backs out again and takes up his post by the control panel, ready to open the train doors.

Phil yawns once more. He can't wait to get home to bed. He almost wishes he were there already, but for one thing.

Lichfield City 07.58

As the train stops, Phil watches the commuters eagerly rush towards the doors and then wait for him to open them.

He does so and steps down onto the platform, scanning their backs and faces. She should be here somewhere. She always catches this train, every time he's done this shift.

But today he can't see her.

Nearly everyone is on now. Disappointed, he steps back through the doors.

Then he notices her. She is standing, her back to him, at the entrance to the next carriage. His eyes slide down her long black hair, neat tailored jacket, grey pinstripe suit and long, smooth stockinged legs – at least he hopes they are smooth not hairy, stockings not tights.

He gets back on the train, closes the doors and continues down the carriage, apparently conscientiously checking every ticket. In reality, he's trying to prepare what he's going to say.

He enters her carriage. She is sitting near the far end, facing in the opposite direction.

He continues asking for tickets, moving metre by metre closer to her seat.

Shenstone 08.02

"Tickets, please," he asks her, looking for a way in through her mahogany eyes.

But she is gazing into the distance and doesn't even look up at his face as she pulls out her pass from her purse and hands it to him. He takes it from her eagerly, too eagerly to have time to think about how he is doing it. He misses her hand by an inch. Instead of warm flesh, his fingers cling to wrinkled plastic covering a photo of her face.

He doesn't even glance at this. He knows from previous journeys that it doesn't compare with the reality, turning what he considers her stunning nose, eyes and lips into ordinary features with no warmth or life. He doesn't look at the pass next to the photocard, either. He knows what it says – her name Catherine Phillips, her date of birth, etc. What he doesn't know is what to say.

"Nice day"? But it isn't. "Awful weather, isn't it?" Too British, too formal, too boring. "Busy day?" Too nosy. "Work, eh, who needs it!" Yes, that's it, some joke or light-hearted comment with a smile or an amusing sigh. He opens his mouth to speak.

But no words come out. His eyes are mesmerised by the blue, teardrop-shaped pendant that dangles above the open neck of her cream blouse. He drags his glance free and his eyes drift downwards to where her skirt ends, an inch above her knees.

Why are his eyes doing this? His thoughts turn his face warm as he realises how long he's been staring at her. It feels like hours. She must have noticed.

But she still isn't looking at him. Her eyes are fixed firmly, unblinking, staring straight in front of her.

He hesitates for a second and then hands the pass back to her, too flustered now to try to make hand or eye contact.

He has missed his chance. He chastises himself as he continues down the carriage. He calls automatically, "tickets,

please," as his hands take, mark and return the tickets presented, without even seeing them or the passengers proffering
them, their bodies swaying from side to side like toy figures
mounted on tiny springs. His body, too, moves with the not-
completely-unpleasant hum of the train's engine, broken now
and then by its rackety-rack jolting along the rails.

In the carriage a mobile phone rings, another beeps, people
talk. Phil hears them but lets the noises slip through his head
without honing in. The background sounds are as familiar
now to his thoughts and senses as the faded green paint on his
bedroom walls.

Blake Street 08.05

Phil opens the doors, and more commuters get on. He
closes them and turns back to Catherine's carriage. He must
check the tickets of the new passengers.

But no one is still standing up. They must all have sat down
already. He recognises none of the faces except hers. He has
no idea whose tickets he has already checked.

He moves towards Catherine and stops at the man opposite. He is dressed in a navy suit with a name badge pinned to
one lapel. Phil can't remember if he has already asked him for
his ticket but he knows he has checked Catherine's. He can't
ask her again without embarrassment and this is the nearest
he can get without doing so.

He takes the man's ticket. There is pen scribble on it. He
must have checked it before. But the man doesn't protest so
he carries on pretending to examine it while looking at
Catherine.

She too is looking at him, he notes excitedly, staring
intently in front of her. Now is his chance to speak to
her, make a joke, some throw-away comment. He moves
slightly. Her eyes do not follow, but remain fixed in front of
her. She hasn't noticed him at all. Her eyes are looking right

through him as if unaware he's even there. He circles the man's ticket in blue biro and moves on.

Butlers Lane 08.07

As the train stops, Phil looks back down the carriage towards Catherine. She is still staring in front of her. He realises that it wasn't him she was looking at, but the man opposite, the guy with the name badge and dark brown hair.

Phil closes the doors and moves on down the train. He must check the tickets in the other carriages, not just hers.

He moves mechanically down the next aisle, fingers flitting from tickets to biro, from cash to his ticket machine.

He wonders if Catherine is still staring at that man back in her carriage. The man's dark brown haircut looks recent, fashionable no doubt. He looks tall, too, and confident, the kind of man Phil would like to be. Maybe then Catherine would stare at him. He wishes she would. Why isn't he more noticeable? He isn't that bad-looking, is he? He's not that old either. Thirty-eight isn't over the hill. It is maturely youthful.

But then no wonder she doesn't look at him. He hasn't done anything to make her look at him. He should have smiled at her more, said something, made her laugh.

Four Oaks 08.10

They have just left the station when a train travelling in the opposite direction passes the window and is gone, like a fleeting image in a half-waking dream.

He has missed his chance again. Phil doesn't understand why it keeps happening. He can talk to other people. He can tell jokes, get a laugh and a smile. Why can't he talk to her?

He has discussed this with his hypnotherapist, Gina. She is a big, laughing lady with a rucksack of anecdotes. He isn't sure whether these are part of his treatment, a way of getting him to relax, or simply because she finds it hard to stop talking. But it's interesting listening to her, and it does put him at ease before she sends him into what feels like a pleasantly relaxing, dreamlike state. They are trying to tackle his anxiety problems and he has been going to her for two hours a week for the past eleven weeks. The hypnotherapy should have started working by now, but it doesn't seem to be helping him today.

Sutton Coldfield 08.13

The train pulls out of the station. Phil feels himself pulled back towards Catherine's seat.

A short, young woman with bleached hair has sat down next to her. He must check her ticket.

Looking at Catherine, he walks towards the woman. She pulls out a pass and he pretends to examine it in detail. All he has to do now is make some joke as he hands it back and try to pull the surrounding passengers, including Catherine, into the laughter.

But Catherine is staring out of the window, her mouth a thin, closed line.

He hands the pass back to the woman without saying a word and continues onto the next passenger.

Wylde Green 08.16

Phil can't remember in much detail exactly what Gina says in his sessions once she has hypnotised him. He starts off imagining himself relaxing in his favourite place – a peaceful beach with the warm sun on his face and a light breeze gliding across his skin. He steps down into somewhere different, and at one point there is a broken boiler that he has to mend. There is also a wall with words written on it, words he fears – rejection, embarrassment, scorn, loneliness, failure. He has to knock it down, brick after brick, with big blows. Then he has to rebuild it again and paint new words in bright colours like love, money, happiness, prestige, success, respect. The things he wants, but hasn't got.

113

He comes closest on the last one. All the young schoolkids go quiet when he enters their carriage in his conductor's uniform. That's a kind of respect, isn't it?

He's good at his job, too, even if it isn't what he wanted to be or do. As a child, he always fancied being a train driver and, as a teenager, he spent hours at the station, watching noisy carriages roar past, ticking them off in his railway books. He even dreamed of going overseas, trying the TGV in France, the ICE in Germany, the bullet train in Japan. That was in the days when he believed he could be or do anything. Sometimes part of him still does believe it, or tries to. A train conductor and a train driver, they're the same sort of job. It's the next best thing, isn't it?

Chester Road 08.17

But it still isn't a train driver. In fact, train conductors and train drivers are not at all the same thing. Phil knows this really. And, though he's no longer interested in trainspotting, he still hasn't managed to travel further from home than Scotland.

He wonders what the man in the suit opposite Catherine does. The name badge is funny, otherwise he looks like a young businessman, important, successful, well-paid – the kind of guy Catherine, or any woman, would want to be with. Not the sort that has the 'women troubles' the other conductors sometimes chat about, or no women at all like Phil. The man certainly looks like he would earn loads, have his choice of women if he wanted, and would get a lot of respect from everyone around him.

Young schoolkids are where the respect ends for Phil. They don't have to be very old before they've learnt contempt, and he certainly doesn't get any respect from the teenagers. They're always talking back to him, with a good excuse for not having a ticket and sometimes even a mouthful of abuse.

He should have done something different – gone to university, used his A-levels for something. He could have backpacked, like Gina, and seen the world. He would love to have been to some of the places she's visited. She makes him laugh with the tales she tells, like the time when she was backpacking and tried to get a train to Budapest, but ended up in Bucharest. She's off again in a few weeks, if she can find someone to travel with. She's been talking about it for ages. He can't help envying her free spirit and her get-up-and-go. Talking with her makes him feel full of energy and life, even after a tedious nine-hour shift.

Phil looks out the window. The train is nearing Erdington, and somehow he is back at the end of Catherine's carriage. He looks over at her. She is slumped back in her seat, gazing at the air in front of her.

As the train pulls into the station, the man opposite her, the one with the name badge, starts to get up. Phil can't remember what was on his ticket. This must be his stop. Phil smiles.

Erdington 08.19

The man sits down again as Phil opens the train door.

Phil closes them again, disappointed. It's not, of course, that he feels threatened by the man's presence next to Catherine, but if he had got off, someone else might have sat opposite her. Then he would have had to go and check their ticket.

"Did you say Graham?" A woman in the corner of the carriage is talking on her mobile phone. Other meaningless phrases float over. "I don't believe you! What did he do then?"

Phil listens. They are fragments of lives that mean nothing to him. He wonders if he and his life seem as distant to other people – if they care as little about his world as he cares about this anonymous woman's and her friends' everyday existences.

Certainly, Catherine doesn't seem to realise he exists.

Gravelly Hill 08.21

Nor does anyone else. He has never had a girlfriend. It's embarrassing, not that anyone knows – except Gina. The hypnotherapy is supposed to be helping build his skills with the opposite sex.

The train is in the city now. They pass factory buildings, traffic, a scrapyard of old cars. It is full of odd bits of iron that nobody wants, the remnants of old vehicles no one can be bothered to repair, not considering them worthy of that much love or attention.

Phil is beginning to feel like one of these breakdowns. He is thirty-eight, too old now for a girlfriend, although Gina says otherwise and continues to say so many times, session after session. But that is only what she says. She is his hypnotherapist after all. That's what he would expect her to say – it's her job, though they often seem to spend the sessions chatting away like old friends.

But no matter how confident and good he feels with Gina, when he leaves his sessions that heavy feeling comes back. He knows he is doomed to live on his own for the rest of his life or, worse still, stuck with his mum. He should have left home long ago, not caved in when his flatshare fell through and his mum started talking about how lonely she was.

Aston 08.25

Outside the train, the landscape becomes urban art – graffiti on a bridge, graffiti on grey boxes beside the track, graffiti on the black, moss-speckled walls. Most of it has been written or painted in white, the symbolic innocence of the colour in ironic contrast to some of the profanities scribbled in it. A few words stand out among the mass of indecipherable hieroglyphics. The rest of the scrawling looks like signatures – some kids' desperate attempt to make their mark on the world.

Phil knows it's vandalism, the sort that, like the scratches on the train windows, takes effort and money to remedy, but part of him still envies their boldness. He too would like to leave his mark on the world. What's the harm in that, in wanting to be noticed, appreciated? He hesitates to put into his thoughts the third word that he has left out, but he knows 'loved' is what Gina would have added.

The train horn sounds and suddenly Phil feels stronger. He knows what Gina would say. He doesn't need a spray-gun to make a mark on his hypnotherapy wall.

Duddeston 08.28

Phil turns away from the window and hurries back towards Catherine. They are nearly at New Street; he has wasted too many minutes. He has no time to lose.

He has just stepped into her carriage when a man in a grey overcoat stops him.

"Excuse me, when's the next train to Cardiff?"

"Cardiff?" Phil stutters.

"Do I change at New Street?"

"New Street? New Street?" Phil hurries to try and understand the words, his eyes and mind on Catherine.

"No, no, University, not New Street." he fidgets with his shirt cuff. "Um, yes, I'm not sure which train, but they'll have the timetable there."

"Thank you." The man smiles, but seems in no hurry to move out of Phil's way.

Phil looks past him to Catherine. She is still looking directly in front of her, staring at or through the passenger opposite.

"Excuse me." Phil starts to edge his way past the person in the overcoat, but then he remembers. He has to do the announcement.

He hurries back to his microphone.

"Birmingham New Street, this is your next station stop…"

He finishes breathlessly a minute later and rushes back towards Catherine.

But when he gets there, she is already at the other end of the carriage, waiting for the doors to open, a queue of passengers behind her.

Birmingham New Street 08.31

The train comes to a standstill, and Phil has to open the doors. He steps onto the platform and looks down the train.

Catherine is standing, statue-like, at the door to her carriage while the other commuters push past her, cursing under their breath. She looks sad, in need of someone to comfort her.

Phil feels he ought to go to her. He realises he needs to act now, instantly, so he can make the most of her inaction. But he can't get his legs to function.

She starts to move, steps off the train and heads away from him towards the exit.

She is going. He has only seconds before she is out of sight.

But she has not gone yet. There is still a chance.

"Never give up." He hears Gina's words as his feet lurch along the platform after Catherine. There is no time like the present and if he doesn't do it this time, what will he tell Gina?

The thought disturbs him. If he does do it, he won't get to tell Gina anything. He won't have any reason to carry on the hypnotherapy. His feet slow at this realisation. Besides, he reasons to himself, Catherine is nearly at the escalator now. There's no point trying to catch her. She has almost gone anyway.

Then, suddenly, she stops and starts walking back, towards him.

"Excuse me," she says. "I can't find my gloves. I think I

must have dropped them on the train."

"I haven't seen them," he replies immediately, thinking perhaps that was why she was looking sad earlier. "Were they expensive or important?"

Now he doesn't feel that he needs to, Phil finds he can talk to Catherine without any problem at all. "We're due out of the station in a minute, but I can have a look later and let you know tomorrow if you're on the same train?" he asks, though he already knows the answer.

As Catherine nods, he tries to cheer her up by adding merrily: "You never know what you'll find where or when!"

She nods again and smiles briefly at him. He smiles in return and continues smiling as he watches her walk away to the escalator. Then he turns back to his train, his thoughts on backpacking and the transport system in Bulgaria. He wonders what it's like. Gina is off there in a few weeks; she has been looking for someone to go with her and he has always wanted to travel.

Thursday

By
Lea Hurst

Thursday

Every day was not the same, insisted Maisie. She had made a serious effort to get rid of the dull blur that Bill's death had caused three years ago. Of course it was never easy, but she reached for her notepad and with quiet determination worked on her Thursday list.

There was shopping, of course. She called it her 'sly-shop'. Ann, her daughter-in-law, always called for her on the first Friday of the month and swept her off to the vast hypermarket at the edge of town where together they hauled bulging trolley loads in and out to the car. When they got back to Maisie's, Ann would check the cupboards for the tinned goods supply and help her pack the freezer in date order so that nothing was wasted or ignored.

But Thursday, for Maisie, was the day when she got herself along to the smaller supermarket in the town and bought biscuits, cola and snacks for her two grandsons. Ann and Pete were settled and prospering – she could not fault either of them in their care of her. She knew of friends whose offspring rushed about and tried to make up for their absence with noisy gestures. But there was a certain wilfulness within her. It might be described as independence, but Maisie knew it simply as determination to do just what she fancied – whether it made sense or not.

She was enjoying her coffee and remembering that she must leave a note for the milkman to deliver juice. She ticked off 'clean cooker' and got up to check the cat food box. She was just picking up the last crumbs of the chocolate bar she had enjoyed with her coffee when the doorbell rang.

"Hello Mum, surprise, surprise."

"Ann dear, I wasn't expecting you."

"I had to go up to the school to pay for the boys' outing – they went without the cheque and I knew the school was desperate. Thought I'd call in and see if you needed anything."

Maisie made Ann a coffee and they settled themselves in the sitting room so Ann could tell Maisie all about the outing and how she had been asked to go with them to help the staff and how she wasn't sure that she wanted to, given that she was already a parent helper with the Year 1 Reading Group and she was being roped in again to organise the tombola for the fair. "'The fayre' as they call it," she said with a laugh.

Maisie stared softly at the wallpaper and listened. Pete had recently painted the kitchen, the bathroom and the hallway of the bungalow, but this room had stayed the same.

The honeysuckle...then the roses...then the trellis and ivy...or should it be the other way 'round. Honeysuckle...

Ann continued brightly with more news.

"Hazel says she is going to see about a trip to Amsterdam for the bulb festival – doesn't that sound lovely?"

...then the trellis...and then...

"She's treating her mother to a weekend break."

Maisie let her eyes jump from the wallpaper at the bottom of the bay window to the piece at the top. She knew the pattern didn't follow on properly.

"Now you're over that rotten cold, you ought to try and get out more. Pete and I worry that you don't get much fun out of life these days."

They'd been short of a roll of wallpaper. It'd taken them ages to agree on the pattern and then Bill got cross with her because she'd left the measurements behind on the kitchen table and they'd had to make a rough calculation there and then in the shop. And it was expensive – "Well worth it for the quality", the salesman had said, addressing Maisie directly. Bill had caught the glance and ordered up there and then.

"We'll patch it round the bay window; no one will ever notice," he'd said and no one ever did. Maisie smiled.

Now she alone knew.

"Have you had any luck getting that new blouse you said you needed? I thought we might try Bentalls next week. They're having one of their mid-season sale things. What do you think?"

Maisie, sitting squarely, watched her hand smoothing the velvet on the arm of the old settee. As it moved, her watch worked itself out from under the cuff of her cardigan. The watch, Bill's watch, winked at her. She moved her wrist round and back, feeling how the links in the band could expand and nip on her skin.

And she was back there, on a long gone day. At the coast, in the sand hills. The old tartan rug laid across the sand and the stumps of marram grass. She had buried her face in Bill's neck, and the wind and sand had blown wild. The metal of the watch strap had scratched at the skin of her thigh. A tiny echo of the stinging rose up and spread across her legs and belly.

Ann looked up and saw the far-away stare and smile. She gave up.

"I must go now, mum – the plumber's due to service the boiler. I'm going to send Pete round at the weekend to draft-proof that kitchen door."

Maisie, still smiling, watched her go. Her face settled as she tried to think of how to tell the girl, how to say to her: "Stop, just stop. I know you mean well, but stop; there's a love."

These days she found pleasure in stillness. She could sit in limbo for ages until, with a grumble, she realised that she was an old fool and had let herself get stiff and cramped. She passed, with little effort, through the duties of her day – feeding the cat, changing the doilies on the dressing table, moving Bill's photo a little to avoid the afternoon sun. During all these tasks she remained untroubled.

It was only when asked to play the role of the busy widow that she felt something like annoyance. The prospect of tutting over lukewarm sausage rolls or growing flushed over a hand of cards – it made her narrow her eyes and brush away at the vision with a flap of her hand. Forever busy they were, getting in and out of coaches or gift shops, organising you to make sandwiches or sweeping out the church hall. It always seemed to coincide with a day when Maisie wanted to sit in the garden and drift.

That's what the 'Thursday list' was really all about.

"I'm afraid I'm busy on Thursdays," she had trained herself to say. She added 'second-hand bookshop' to the list and wondered again why she liked trailing around those sagging shelves so much more than going to the local library. Next door to it, a charity shop had opened. They were always good for a browse – a little fritter perhaps. The list sufficient, she could get ready to go out.

The spring sunshine had started to move away from the kitchen and the light in the bathroom next to it looked thin and chilly. Maisie braced herself and, still irritated by Ann's cajoling, threw off her old morning clothes. She watched the hot water bolt into the bathtub and threw in a good slosh of the bubblebath she kept for her grandsons. She smiled back at Billy-Bubbles in his purple pot and tested the temperature. Calm returned, and pleasure, as she soaked, sponged, dried and powdered.

Warmed through, she shuffled to the bedroom next door for clean clothes. Crossing the room she stopped suddenly at the wardrobe and stared at herself in the full-length mirror. She scanned her face, her hand to her mouth. Then quickly, she looked over her old, withering body. Not much to be said about that – it's to be expected, it's what happens. With gentle deliberation she unlocked the wardrobe door and took down Bill's old tweed overcoat. The watch and this coat she had kept. She buried her face in it and smiled at the smokey roughness. A tall man, he had often hugged her to it, her cheek pressed in against the horn buttons. She slipped into it and swung the long, heavy sleeves around herself – could she still feel his arms? Old fool. She watched herself for a moment and then carefully buttoned the coat and folded back the thick cuffs. The collar, where the silk lining joined the tweed, rasped at the wrinkled skin on her neck and breasts. As she moved around the room the long folds flapped round her legs. She shivered when the cold silk touched her skin. This feels real she thought. Not the silly fancy of winning a draw prize at a bazaar or guessing the weight of a cake. The tweed and the silk together, she was touching him and she was alive. Back at the mirror, her cheeks had flushed a little and her eyes seemed brighter. She picked up her purse and list from the kitchen and went through to the back door where she had left her old flat shoes.

She swung her way along towards the shops, her hands deep in the silk pockets. She spotted a bustling church acquaintance, some distance away, and swore softly at the inevitable meeting. Not necessarily, she decided, and with cheerful disregard she walked, head down, across to the other side of the road. It was a small wickedness and Maisie fluttered with its triumph. But she had wasted warmth and energy on it and catching sight of herself in a shop front, all coat and thin bare legs, she suddenly felt exposed and foolish. She hesitated, then pressed on.

By the time she reached the supermarket, her pace had slowed; her mind had settled again into softness. She hunched herself further down into the coat and hung a wire basket over one arm. Vague-eyed she began to move down the first aisle. She selected a raisin loaf from the 'specials shelf' and met the eyes of a toddler in his trolley seat. He struggled round and offered her the biscuit he was chewing. She smiled after him as he was whisked away by the busy mother. He was still looking at her as the trolley turned the corner.

She almost gave up on her search for Jammy Dodgers. Energy bars, wholewheat organic snacks, every kind of built-in goodness. Then she saw them on the very top shelf. Unbalanced, but determined, Maisie struggled and flicked a packet from the edge of the row into her hand, tipping it into her basket. She paused as her wrist protested at the effort.

The next aisle was busy but she made steady progress towards the cat food, her eyes down, watching the toes of her shoes as they appeared and disappeared from under the swinging hem of the coat. Halfway down a woman with a laden trolley suddenly turned a full circle, totally blocking all progress. The long shawl she was wearing required readjustment and she swirled it across her shoulder. The fringing brushed against Maisie's face and her eyes blinked hard. It made her gasp.

"No, no! Free range," a sharp-voiced cry cut across her path. "Yes, get a dozen."

It was a young couple, one instructing the other and talking on a mobile phone while trying to check the eggs for breakages.

Maisie frowned and tried to reach for her list in the depths of the coat pocket. She fancied a change for her supper. What was it she had decided on?

Perhaps fish, she thought, and turned towards the bank of large freezer chests.

She reached across to the back for a tempting readymade luxury fish pie. As she pulled at them, the chilled air crept in at the neck of the coat. It caught her by surprise and the packet fell from her hands onto the floor. An attendant, stacking a shelf nearby, picked it up for her, but Maisie turned away.

"Your fish, madam", he called after her, but with a shake of her head she scuttled to the end of the aisle, desperately fiddling with the collar of the coat, looking for another button to fasten at the neck. She couldn't find any. She wanted the fish but could not go back. Out of the corner of her eye she saw him still standing, packet in hand, looking after her. She walked on, past breakfast cereals, through bleaches, toilet cleaners and mop heads. The basket hung heavily. She changed hands but felt no better and changed back again.

What was it Ann had said about her grandsons' latest craze? Cheesey Dippers? As she turned at the end of the aisle to head for the dairy products she jolted to a stop, breath caught, eyes wide and fixed. In front of her in the fruit and veg section was a display of early peaches. They blushed and glowed at her, and rooted her to the spot with their loveliness. She reached forward and gently stroked one with the tips of her fingers.

And, effortlessly, she was back in France. The first time they had been abroad. On a twin town weekend twenty-five years ago. They had given themselves a headache trying to drink wine with their lunch of chicken and frites and had decided to have a lie-down instead of going on the afternoon coach trip. Carrying the kilo of peaches they had bought earlier, they'd gone back to their hotel and slept it off. When they woke they made cups of tea in their room and decided to eat the peaches. But the fuzz had tickled their lips and faces and they had tickled each other and rubbed the peaches on their stomachs, wriggling and laughing at their silliness.

Maisie grasped a peach and stared at it – she felt its weight and let it sink into her hand, glowing. She slipped it through into the two-way pocket of the coat, daring herself to rub it against her side. A giggle rose as she thought about it, hold-ing it there, motionless against the wall of her stomach. She could see again the sun slanting through the old lace curtains and hear the squeaky foreign traffic noises floating up from the square. They had called each other silly fools and slurped at the yellow flesh of the peaches.

Her eyes spanned the pyramid of fruit. Could they possibly taste the same, would the juice run, would the flavour sing? They were terribly tempting, but she stared hard at them, pro-tecting herself against false promise. Suddenly she was beyond doubt. She felt her arm stretch out from the coat sleeve. She would have peaches, a kilo at least. She would have them, enough to cover her with their juice, enough to gorge on, enough to choke with love.

Her hand reached again and again, choosing only the largest, the heaviest, the ripest. The basket swayed with their weight, the handle biting into her arm. Her hand went to her chest, clutching at the neck of the old coat. She fought for breath. Maisie tipped forward and, reaching out to steady her-self, found her face only inches from the fruit. She let her breath slow down and deepen, and she closed her eyes, leav-ing only the scent of the peaches. She could sense people near her, passing by, and she opened her eyes and straightened up.

Struggling with both hands on the basket, she braced her-self and walked, eyes front, towards the checkout. There was a snigger somewhere behind her in the queue. She watched the hands of the girl at the till and followed the fruit rolling gently towards a young trainee who packed them into a car-rier bag. She fumbled with the clasp on her purse and paid, without meeting their gaze. The lad lifted the bag down for her. She took it from him, one hand pressed at the front of the coat and, struggling, began to carry her heavy load home.

Just as she was leaving the store, she heard Ann calling

after her, "Mum, mum, why didn't you say you were coming down today – I'd have given you a lift. The car's over here, let me get your shopping. What on earth have you been up to? Oh, peaches, how lovely. Fancy you buying peaches. Good for you, just the treat you need."

Maisie allowed Ann to tuck in the trailing skirt of the coat before closing the car door. When bidden, she did up her seat belt only to realise, with a smile, that the solitary peach still sat heavy in her pocket.

Saturday

By
Miguel Ylareina

Saturday

Sometimes life changes slowly, like the tide wearing away a cliff. Sometimes life changes all at once, like a big section of cliff tumbling into the ocean, revealing something deeper within, something new.

Felissa Johnson rolled into a sitting position on her bed. Her gaze through the window followed the dawn shadows on her mama's blueberry farm and the adjoining land beyond. She arched her fifteen-year-old body, stretching her black skin taut, shaking the sleep from her bones. Something wasn't right. She squinted against the sunlight streaming into the room. Hank Morton's farm, beyond the fence, seemed the same as ever. The neighbouring farmhouse with its black shingle roof was set against white siding, the morning rays dewy in their stillness.

Hank was an old guy who ran the farm next door by himself, though, like her mama, he hired blueberry pickers and a manager to harvest the fruit in season. She thought of his spry walk, his shock of white hair, and his freckled skin.

It was the shed. Something was wrong with Hank's shed. The door had something painted on it that Felissa couldn't make out. It looked like a teardrop about the size of a basketball. She opened her window a little, lifting the sash. A mild scent of roses wafted up from below. Her mama, Faith Johnson, loved red roses and took care of them with nostalgic tenderness. Felissa thought of her, trimming rose hips after the petals had floated one by one onto the soft earth below. Her mama loved to snip a large bunch of flowers and set their heavy scent hanging with sentimental glory in the graceful dining room below her daughter's bedroom.

The teenager's gaze shifted beyond Hank's rows of blueberry bushes to the cherry orchard beside it. The old farmer would soon be up and about, surveying his crops. Every day he bestowed his love on the rows of fruit bushes, watering, fertilising and spraying them. He also kept an eye on the cherry trees with their as yet unripe orbs hanging delicately. Hank had lived there forever, long before Felissa's time.

She stared again at the shed door. It looked like someone had crudely painted a noose onto the ancient, weathered wood. Why would anyone do that? Hank was a white man and Felissa and her mama were black, but he was no racist. He was the kindest soul imaginable – always polite, helping out if needed, but never intrusively. He was a neighbour in the truest sense of the word.

A slow movement caught Felissa's attention in the orchard. There was a boy up one of the cherry trees. She knew it must be Lorman, visiting for the summer like he always did. He must have got to Hank's late last night. They hadn't seen each other since last summer. She'd played with the boy for so many years, since they were little kids. They played hide-and-seek among the blueberry bushes, played tag in the orchard, and climbed trees and talked about whatever came to mind. Lorman had always been easy to talk to. His dirty blonde hair was usually short, but always long enough to flick across his forehead in a cute sort of way. His arms and legs were wiry with a taut muscularity that developed every year. He had brown eyes like her own, and sometimes she used to stare into them, searching for her own reflection.

Coming out of her reverie, Felissa looked again at the mysterious thing on the shed, then rushed away to get dressed. She was quickly into some jeans and a shirt. Dashing by the mirror she caught a fleeting glimpse of her black hair in corn rows, growing into beaded braids, the tassels cascading behind.

****

Felissa rushed down the stairs and into the kitchen where her mama was already drinking sweet black coffee and reading the paper. Today was a big day for them – the first day of the blueberry season.

"Lissa, you up already, girl?" The words were slow and measured, as they often were first thing in the morning. The tone was warm with a hint of ironic humour. Felissa was an early riser like her mama, but 6.30 was earlier than usual.

"Lorman's at Hank's this mornin'. I saw him in the orchard. I thought I'd ask him to help me get the blueberry stand set up for you if he isn't doing anything else."

"Well, thank you honey, that would be wonderful, but please have some breakfast first," smiled Faith. She moved gracefully from the kitchen table to a nearby cupboard to retrieve some dry cereal for her daughter, continuing to the refrigerator for the milk.

Setting an empty bowl and spoon onto the table, Felissa slid into a chair and served herself. A silence descended as her mama returned to the paper. She looked across at the concentrating face, wondering how the day would unfold. That thing on the shed door worried her. Should she tell? It seemed silly before going to investigate. No need to worry her mama on this important day.

It would be very busy. Soon the farm would be swarming with hired blueberry pickers, directed by a foreman who her mama hired every year. Big Jadi always brought a smile to Felissa's face. He was Indian, from Andhra Pradesh state, and had a big smile and an equally big moustache. He always had stories from the Bay of Bengal, where he returned to visit relatives every so often. Big Jadi drove the workers hard, but was fair, and always got the job done in a way that left you thinking he had it easy.

Her eye wandered outside to the rows of bushes with their

tiny fruit. Most of the blueberries went to wholesalers, but some were sold at a seasonal fruit stand at the edge of the farm. There was usually enough traffic coming by at this time of year to keep her mama busy running things.

Felissa sighed. What drove her mama, year after year? Why did she stay on the farm? It was hard work and a lot of pressure. Her mama held down a full-time job as a nurse at the hospital, too, working twelve-hour shifts for four days, then three days off. This time of year, though, she took time off to supervise farm activities. It was hard for Felissa growing up without a papa. She'd hardly known him. When she was three years old, he'd been killed in an accident. Before that, there had been a big chicken farm, too, but now there were was just a few chickens in the barn.

It was always too quiet for the teenager. She thought it was unfair that she had to live on a farm, alone with her mama, with no brothers or sisters. It seemed wrong to be stuck out here instead of living in town where the action was. She had school friends that were forever talking about their boyfriends, shopping, TV shows, and about their favourite young stars. Maybe she didn't miss them all that much. She wondered if she was too much like a boy. Lorman was a better friend to her, closer than the girls in town. He was quiet on the whole, but could be very talkative and animated when you got him going. They were always competitive with each other. She wondered if he'd be able to out race her this year.

Through the kitchen window, she saw her friend heading towards the house, and noticed he was taller than last year. He was coming over very early. Something was wrong. Was it about that mark on the shed door? Her pulse quickened and a swallow stuck like soft glue in her mouth.

Lorman gave a knock on the kitchen door, which she opened.

"Hey Liss, how's it going? Hmm, cool hair you got there. Hi Mizz J. Sorry to drop by at this time of day. Grandpa left for town an hour ago."

Faith turned, ignoring for now the information about her neighbour, and regarded the young man with interest.

"Well, hello Lorman." Her expression was kind and interested. "Had a good year? Looks like you've been eating your Wheaties."

Lorman blushed ever so slightly. "Oh, well, thank you ma'am, I had a busy spring. I was packing groceries at the local store and of course there was school work, baseball, and an old Chevy I'm starting to fix up too."

"Well, that's just fine Lorman. You know, I want to hear all about it at the proper time, but Lissa here was mentioning to me a few minutes ago that she might ask you for some help. I need you both to get the blueberry stand ready. That is if Hank doesn't have anything else for you just now."

"I'd be glad to help out, ma'am, but I have to tell you, I'm worried about grandpa. He drove off real early this morning. I've never known him to do without breakfast before going into town. He told me to keep an eye on the farm and to leave a message for him at Harkners Hardware if anything unusual happened. He looked worried, but he didn't tell me what it was all about. I can't believe he still hasn't bought a mobile phone."

Felissa exchanged looks with her mama. Something froze her insides like slush. If Hank was gone, it had to be about the shed for sure. What was inside it anyway? What could that paint on the door mean? She'd talk to Lorman about it. Her mama might be scared. After all, it did look like a noose. What could it all lead to? A lynching? Why else would there be a noose? She closed her eyes and tried to control her breathing. This was the twenty-first century. There weren't lynchings anymore and, besides, that happened to men. She shuddered. Surely it wasn't someone with something against Big Jadi?

She looked at her mama, who considered before replying to the young man. "You're right, that's not like Hank. He's getting up there these days, isn't he? Seventy-five? I hope he's feeling all right. It would be just like him to go off to the doctor's without mentioning it. I tell you what, Lorman. I've got Mr. Jadi coming in a few minutes to organise the workers and a couple of van loads of blueberry pickers soon after that. I'll keep an eye on things at Hank's if you help Lissa with the stand. Oh, and could you two feed the chickens first? Lissa knows what needs setting out at the berry stand and how to arrange the signs and things. I think you do too. I'm aiming to open about 9:30 so you can take your time, but I'd rather have it all ready soon."

****

Felissa watched Lorman ahead of her as they made their way to the barn. It was a small barn, built in the traditional way with a red roof and white trim. They got out the chicken feed and poured enough for the few chickens, who flocked to the feed dish squawking and pecking. It smelled of hay and poultry – not unpleasant, but thick.

Felissa felt tight inside, as though something bad was going to happen, but she didn't know how to bring it up to Lorman. Instead she made small talk, renewing their friend-ship after another year, chatting about baseball, cars and music.

They quickly moved outside again, making their way to the front of the property by the road to the fruit stand. It was a wooden structure on the edge of a makeshift gravel parking lot. A large sign over the entrance with the single word 'Blueberries' marked the stand's main product, although Faith usually sold a few vegetables and some home-made jam as well. A big 'CLOSED' sign also hung at the entrance. They'd need to take that down. The stand was divided in half, one section where small containers were filled with blueberries, weighed into varying sizes, and a larger section where rectangular cardboard boxes were displayed, each containing twenty pounds of berries. These came straight in from the fields, as the workers picked into them. There wasn't any fruit as yet, but it wouldn't take long before large quantities came pouring in, starting with the first boxes that Big Jadi would carry in after the initial couple of hours of picking.

Taking a deep breath, Felissa felt her insides tighten. She couldn't explain her curiosity and terror, but it was bursting inside, and she finally let it out in a torrent.

"I saw you up a cherry tree this morning."

"You did?"

"It was when I got up. There was this leg swinging. I knew it was you."

She thought she noticed her friend flinch a little. Maybe he didn't like the thought of being watched.

"Yeah," he said. "I was up there thinking. It was weird with grandpa leaving and all." Lorman shifted empty baskets around, ready to weigh berries into.

"What do you mean, weird?" Felissa was helping, but listlessly, less energetic than usual. She caught Lorman looking at the fear in her eyes.

"Grandpa was totally different this morning than last night. He picked me up at the airport and we drove to the farm as usual. We talked about baseball and my pitching record, stuff like that. We had a late snack and then went to bed around midnight. This morning it was like he was totally changed.

He was up at 5am. I heard him wandering around outside, whistling, then it stopped, and he came back into the house. I thought he might be getting ready for the start of the season like your mother, but no. He was so quiet when I came downstairs; he had this far-away look in his eyes. I couldn't tell what was going on. He looked kind of mad, or sad. It was hard to work it out. Maybe afraid, even. I asked him what it was, but he just said he had to go into town for a while and he figured he'd be back later in the morning."

"So then you went out into the orchard?"

"I was sort of freaked out, but I had some breakfast and then went out and wandered around the farm like I always do on the first day when I get here. Next thing I know, I'm by that shed where grandpa planted all those roses a couple of years ago. There was this white paint on the door that wasn't there last year. I wasn't sure what it was. It looks kind of like an 'O' with a tail at the top, or a rain or teardrop. How long has it been there, Liss?"

"It wasn't there yesterday." Her voice betrayed a tremble.

"Oh, man. Well, why would anyone paint a weird-looking raindrop there? Would grandpa? It doesn't make sense."

"I don't think that's what it is", suggested Felissa. She turned to face Lorman, who had just put down a stack of cardboard baskets near the scales used to weigh fruit.

"So what do you think it is?"

"A noose. It's making me scared."

Felissa didn't feel like herself. She was usually fearless with just about everything. When they were little kids exploring together, she was always the first to wade into the creek, or to climb a high tree branch. She wasn't afraid of insects either. But this was different. This wasn't about striking out into the new, it was the unknown coming to her.

"Did you go into the shed? What's in it?"

"It was locked. That's another thing I was thinking about when I was sitting in the tree. He's had that shed locked for a while, a few years I think. What could he be keeping in there?"

Something about Hank locking the shed made Felissa's stomach churn. It made her curious, too, in a horrible kind of way, like she wanted to know, but also didn't.

"Aw Liss, you know my grandfather even better than me. I bet he's worried about something – I'm just not sure what."

"We have to get into that shed to find out."

Lorman's face turned from a blueberry basket to Felissa.

"What? We can't just break in there. I mean, we shouldn't..." His voice trailed off as he looked back beyond his friend's house to Faith's rows of blueberries and his grandfather's beyond that.

"For one thing, Faith or Mr. Jadi would catch us trying to get in."

"No they won't. They'll be busy with the workers and getting them into the fields, preparing to write down what everyone's pickings are, things like that." Felissa's voice was adamant.

"What if he has something alive in there that he doesn't want to be let out?"

"What?" Felissa hadn't considered this possibility.

"I don't know, maybe he trapped something and has it holed up in the shed until he can haul it somewhere else, or get somebody else to do it."

"You mean like a skunk?"

"Or a coyote, or a fox or something." Lorman looked as if he was starting to convince himself.

"Look", said Felissa in an exasperated tone. "I'm going to get my flashlight and find out what's in there. For one thing, none of that explains the mark on the door." She watched

Lorman's reaction, knowing this was the showdown moment. She didn't think she could stand up to him if he really wanted to try and stop her. After all, the shed wasn't on her farm; it was on Hank Morton's. It was trespassing, really. But Felissa had a bad feeling about that shed and nothing was going to stop her from getting to the bottom of this. She wouldn't be content until the secret was out. Lorman shrugged and put his hands in his pockets.

"Okay, okay, get your flashlight, but you explain to me how we're gonna pull this off. If we get caught, this is your idea, not mine." His tone was resigned.

"I know. But Lorman, I have to find out." Her voice was pleading. "What if your grandpa's in trouble? You have to help. I'll watch out for anyone coming while you figure out how to get inside. What's covering the shed window?"

"There a blind inside, but with a flashlight we should be able to see what's in there, at least some of it."

They were almost finished with the fruit stand. Lorman got out some sandwich boards advertising the berries, which would be put out further down the road once things opened for business, and the big 'OPEN' sign that Big Jadi would put up.

Felissa had so many questions. Surely Hank wasn't some kind of racist? He didn't seem like one. Her mama would have known about that. Faith had grown up on this farm with her mama, Granny Brown, whose husband had been killed in an accident just like Felissa's dad. She was fuzzy about how they'd come to actually own the farm. She thought it might have all belonged to Hank at one time, but she wasn't sure. Their neighbour had always seemed so...normal. Nothing strange or even mildly scary had ever happened until today. Perhaps he'd been a member of the Klan when he was young? Felissa doubted it, but now she wasn't sure of anything. She turned to Lorman as they walked from the blueberry stand towards her house.

"Okay, I'm going inside for a second to get the flashlight. Meet me over at your grandpa's place by the shed."

"All right. I hope grandpa's okay," Lorman mumbled.

He shuffled off towards the low fence that separated the farm properties. Felissa slipped inside the house and found the flashlight her mama kept in a cupboard. She looked out the kitchen window and saw Big Jadi had just arrived in his truck. A van full of blueberry pickers had come too and they were getting out near the field. Not wanting to be seen, Felissa slipped out the front door, ran across the driveway and rushed past some low trees to the other side of the barn. She made her way behind it, where she hopped over the fence, breathless more from anticipation than exertion.

Lorman was already beside the shed. There was a single window on the side where he was standing. The door was on the opposite end, facing Felissa's house. He peered inside with a flat hand across his eyebrows.

"Do you see anything?" asked Felissa.

"It seems pretty dark in there. Here, give me the flashlight and I'll take another look. Keep a look out for grandpa's truck all right?"

"Don't worry, I will."

Felissa watched as Lorman aimed the beam of light along the edge of the window. Inside, the blind didn't fully conceal the contents of the room. They looked up and down and around for a few seconds, and then Lorman stared straight ahead, looking in. It seemed like there was a bench on one side and a cabinet on the other.

"What?" Felissa thought he'd found something.

"Nothing. I'm trying to figure out how to get in without breaking the lock on the door. I don't want to do that."

"Is the window locked?"

"No, but it's really old. I think it's permanently stuck in place."

"Could you try lifting it up with that cross-piece of wood halfway up?" Felissa looked at Lorman's arms. They were strong for a sixteen-year-old. She felt something rise in her at the sight and turned to look at him. How could he ever really understand what it meant to be black? She could see he didn't share her fright, her sick feeling, wondering what they'd find. She was glad they were together and that she wasn't doing this by herself.

Lorman spoke to her in return.

"I tried that when you were in the house. I can't budge the window up. It won't move. If I knew where grandpa kept a crowbar or something like…"

"My mama has one," interrupted Felissa. "It's in the barn. Hold on, I'll be right back."

She trotted back to the fence and over, slowing to a walk on the other side. Suddenly she saw Big Jadi emerging from the barn doors just beyond her. She had the feeling of being caught red-handed, but she didn't want to stop now. She looked at him. He probably wouldn't stop for long, so she took the initiative.

"Hiya Mr. Jadi. How ya doin'?"

"Oh, hi Lissa. I'm great. In fact I'm downright wonderful, now that the season has started. This is one of my favourite times of year down here on the farm. Just smell that air!" His thick, deep voice was like a tiger's purr.

"It's a barn, Mr. Jadi." She grinned back at him, though there was no smile in her heart.

"Exactly. Take a good deep breath. You'll probably end up working in an office somewhere most of your life and will never get to savour anything like this again. I can't tell you the times I wish I 'preciated what I had back home. Anyway, your mama's driving me hard, so I better get back to it. See you 'round."

"See ya."

Felissa had hardly been listening to the conversation. She had been looking at his moustache and her mind was on the crowbar hung at the back of the tool cupboard in the barn. As soon as Big Jadi was around the corner, she made a run for the cupboard, found the tool she was looking for, and scampered back to the door of the barn. Looking both ways and not seeing anyone, she ran back to the fence, climbed over it and brought the prize to Lorman.

The heavy steel bar slid easily into a space below the shed window. There were four panes of glass framed in the wood sash; two of these were in a lower section which was designed to be lifted and two in an upper section that was permanently fixed in place. The frame showed signs of having once been painted, but it had been so long since that time that it consisted of almost entirely bare, weathered wood. Lorman hesitated. He didn't like stepping into the rose-bed where his grandpa delighted in raising beautiful roses.

Felissa pursed her lips. She figured she knew what he was thinking. The window was old and might break. That wasn't important right now. What was important was finding out what was locked away in there.

"C'mon, see if it'll open."

"No, wait. Are you sure? Just a minute, I want to go 'round and look at the door again."

Felissa tugged on his shirt.

"No, I don't want to get caught before we find something out. Let's just do it."

She saw his inner turmoil. She'd never pushed him to do anything like this before. She hoped he could see how important it was to her. Something inside was driving her to keep going. There was danger at hand, concealed, and she wanted to get it out into the open. If there was anything Felissa couldn't stand, it was hidden terror. Perhaps Lorman could wait for Hank to come back, but she couldn't. Her gut told her to keep going.

She felt sorry for Lorman. He just wanted to please everyone. He wanted to make everything all right. Sometimes that was possible, and sometimes it wasn't. Life's like that.

All at once, Lorman heaved down on the crowbar, using the leverage to force the window up. At first there was nothing, no movement whatsoever. The window didn't budge. He narrowed his eyes and held his breath, calling on every hidden reserve of strength, and gave a mighty push.

Suddenly there was the gunning of a truck engine. Felissa and Lorman both gasped and realised it was coming from Faith's farm. At the exact same moment, there was a quick snap and the lower window moved up a couple of inches. They froze. Felissa saw that the truck was Big Jadi's; he was leaving her mama's farm for town.

The teenagers exhaled. Lorman dropped the crowbar and tried to lift the window. As he jerked upwards, it came up, about two inches at a time, until there was an opening large enough to crawl into. Lorman didn't hesitate and pushed the blind in with his hand, put one leg and then the other over the window sill until he was sitting on it, his legs dangling into the shed.

"Hey, Liss, pass me the flashlight," he rasped.

Felissa looked around, spotting the flashlight that had been dropped under a rose bush. A whiff of red rose caught her nose before she stepped over and handed the cylindrical light to her companion in crime. Lorman flipped it on and slid into the shed like a practised limbo dancer, disappearing from view. Felissa heard his voice calling out to her.

"C'mon, don't just hang around out there, come inside!"

"Okay. Here, take this crowbar so it's not out here," replied Felissa as she swung up to get inside too, handing him the cool, hard steel.

She felt her running shoes touch the wooden floor as Lorman grabbed her hand to make sure she didn't fall. Felissa was shaking with anticipation. At the same time, the feel of Lorman's hand closing on hers felt somehow intimate. She was aware of the warmth as she withdrew it, her eyes adjusting to the dim light. The flashlight beam moved around as the friends examined the contents of the shed.

It was spookily dark with the one window shaded by the blind. Her eyes caught an empty work bench with a couple of drawers on one side, but no sign of any tools or implements. Against the other wall was a large piece of furniture that looked like a wardrobe, rising towards the roof of the shed. There was a combination padlock locking the two doors. It had three dials on it.

Lorman looked at Felissa.

"I bet I know what the combination to that thing is. Here, hold this flashlight on it."

Felissa watched as his thumb and middle finger adjusted the combination to 3-3-0. He pulled down on the lock and presto! It opened. She gaped in surprise.

"How did you know that?"

"There was another lock in grandpa's basement once with the same combination."

Felissa felt unsteady. Now that she was inside, it felt claustrophobic. What if someone saw the open window and trapped them in the shed?

Lorman opened the wardrobe doors and Felissa shone the light inside. It looked empty at first, but then they noticed there was a large sack on a high shelf. Felissa felt her heart pounding like an angry fist. She saw the wild look in Lorman's eyes as he reached up to pull the sack down.

He looked afraid of what they might find, but yanked at it until it fell down with a clunk.

"Open it," she said, pointing the flashlight down through the darkness into the brown folds of the sack.

"I am, I am!" he shot back, frantic to end the suspense. There was definitely something pretty heavy inside. Fumbling, he found the opening of the bag and held it out as the spotlight shone into it.

Inside was a thick coil of rope, grey with age. Lorman pulled it out as if it was a hot potato. He dropped it onto the floor.

It was a noose.

****

"Oh God, Oh God, Oh God," gasped Felissa, who had dropped the flashlight onto the floor too. She felt her stomach start to heave as she tried to contain the instinct to vomit. What could this be about? Why was it here? Why did Hank have it locked up? Felissa fell against Lorman who was breathing so hard he was almost hyperventilating.

They were both speechless. Lorman kicked at the rope, sending it to a corner of the shed. Felissa's impulse was to get out of there right away. She moved towards the window as Lorman picked up the flashlight. Though instead of following her, he opened the upper work bench drawer. It was empty. He opened the lower one. Inside was a single yellow envelope.

"Wait," called Lorman, as Felissa had one leg out of the window.

"No, let's get out of here," she called back.

"I've found something else," he said hurriedly as he opened the unsealed envelope. There was a black and white photograph inside. He stared at it wide-eyed, examining it under the flashlight beam and turning it over. As Felissa came back in, Lorman suddenly screwed up his face in revulsion.

"What is it?" she managed, hesitantly.

"Let's get out of here – you don't want to see this," he replied quickly, snapping the photo back into the envelope and tossing it back into the open drawer. She could see a fearful look in his eyes.

As much as Felissa was sick to her stomach, her horrified curiosity got the better of her. She wrenched the flashlight out of Lorman's hand and snatched up the envelope, plucking out the photograph. At first she saw the back of the picture, on which was scrawled in pencil, 'Tom Brown', and in pen, 'Innocent'. On the other side was a picture of a man hanging by his neck from a rope on a tree, surrounded by a number of smug-looking young men. His neck was twisted at a grotesque angle. The group was white, the victim black.

It was her grandfather.

****

Seized by a horrified rush of adrenaline, Felissa threw the picture and envelope back into the drawer, slammed it shut forcefully, and bolted out through the window. Lorman did likewise, following the racing girl to the orchard, past the trees, across a ditch, and into a forested area beyond, where she collapsed, her whole body shuddering and heaving in uncontrollable gasps of pain.

Lorman's skin was drained of colour. He was shaking. His eyes betrayed confusion and uncertainty. He knelt beside her, panting.

Felissa lay on the ground, looking up at him, trying to keep her distance. The feeling of betrayal and loneliness was sinking into her like a heavy fog rolling in from the sea. Slowly, she tried to collect her thoughts. What was real? Who could she trust? Her mama had told her that Tom, her granddad, had died in an accident. Was she hiding the truth or did she not know what had really happened? Were they living beside a murderer? The thought convulsed her stomach. She saw Lorman reaching out to comfort her and she tightened away from him into a foetal ball.

"Just leave me alone!"

"Liss, who was that?"

She rocked back and forth in agony for several minutes. Then she looked straight up through the trees at the sky. At last Felissa glanced at Lorman's eyes, which were diverted from her's, trance-like, blank. It came to her that he didn't know as much as she did. But what did she really know? Hank had to be the killer! Didn't he? Then she thought why did it say 'innocent' on the back of the photograph? What did they think her granddad had done to deserve that wretched, torturous death? There were more questions than answers. The image of the black man's neck in the picture sickened her beyond measure.

In choking, angry words she started to speak to Lorman.

"That was my granddad in that picture. Yours is a murderer."

"What the...?" Lorman turned to her, eyes wide. She could see a million things were suddenly running through his head. He took a few paces, grew red with anger, and grabbed a dead tree branch, swinging it heavily against a tree trunk. The force broke off the end of the branch with a reverberating crack.

She watched his fury reach its zenith as he hammered on

the tree with the remainder of the branch, yelling "No!" again and again. After exhausting himself with the exertion, he sat down on a fallen log close to Felissa. She could smell his sweat. There was no sound, but tears were rolling down his cheeks, falling onto his t-shirt.

After a while they looked at each other in silence. What was there to say?

Finally, Lorman spoke.

"You know, Liss, who painted that noose? I doubt it was grandpa. How could he be a murderer? I don't believe it."

"He knew what happened to my granddad. He's hiding something."

"Why would he keep that stuff in there? I don't understand."

Felissa thought – if her mama didn't know about this, she'd be devastated if she found out. On the other hand if she did know about it, why had she lied about what had happened? Was it the shame? Maybe she was trying to protect her daughter from a harsh reality. What was the truth? Her mama was a tough woman.

Suddenly there was a voice calling from Hank's farm. It was Faith calling her daughter with desperate shouts.

****

Jumping to her feet, Felissa looked at Lorman, scared. Part of her wanted to stay hidden in the trees, but she knew that would make things worse. She steeled herself to confront her mama, her heart burning with anguish. She wasn't sure what she wanted to do, cry on her mama's shoulder, throw a screaming fit, or yell and run.

Lorman followed and they emerged from the woods, jumping over the ditch. Faith was in Hank's orchard, scanning the trees. Felissa could see that her mama had spotted them.

"Lissa, get over here right now. For God's sake, please hurry up! You too, Lorman. I just got a call from Hank. He's in the town. I'm not sure what's going on. It sounded like he was at the police station. He said if a red truck pulls up to close the door and lock ourselves inside, and not to open to anyone. He's never said anything like this before. I hope he hasn't gone off his rocker, but it didn't sound like it."

They all started running to Faith and Felissa's house. The blueberry workers were getting into their vans and leaving the farm.

"Shouldn't you be calling the cops, ma'am?" shouted Lorman as they sprinted along.

"I did," explained Faith, getting breathless, "I called them and then sent all the berry pickers home."

"You did what, mama?"

"Hold your horses, wait until we get inside," said Faith sharply as they mounted the steps.

Inside, Faith closed the drawing room and then the kitchen curtains. Felissa and Lorman huddled at the kitchen table. Lorman looked drawn and tense. Felissa felt her hands shaking and started to chew on her fingernails. Her mama sat down beside them.

"The police put me on hold. When they spoke to me again, they said Hank was down there."

Lorman sat up straight, looking at her intensely.

"Did they say why?" he asked quickly.

"No. All they said was that he was trying to convince them that the farm was in danger. They didn't say anything about a red truck like he did. I don't know what's going on. Oh, by the way," here Faith changed her tone in a severe, rising pitch. "What were you both doing in those trees beyond the farm? Shame on you, Lorman! You were supposed to be watching things for Hank. And shame on you, Lissa, for not telling me where you were going. What kind of sneaking around is going on here?"

"Mama, it was me," returned Felissa, eyes cast down. For a split second she wondered if she should tell the whole truth.

"I saw something," she continued, "on Hank's shed door. Did you see it?"

"I didn't notice a thing," answered Faith, parting the kitchen curtains a little and having a look across her farm to Hank's. "Why, there's something..."

"Yes, mama," cut in Felissa, "Someone painted a noose there. I didn't know what to think about it so I asked Lorman, but he wasn't sure either. He said his grandpa was acting strange. We..."

Here, she stopped, looking at Lorman. She wished he'd tell her mama that they'd broken into Hank's shed, but he was silent. She glared at him while her mama was looking at her expectantly. She suddenly realised how old her mama was looking, her forehead a sea of anxious wrinkles, the folds like little waves flowing down onto one another.

"I wanted to find out what was inside the shed and I got Lorman to break into it." She continued as her mama put her hand to her mouth. "You know what we found in there? We found a sack with a noose in it, and a picture." Suddenly Felissa sounded very accusing. "It was a picture of your papa..." She couldn't bear to say anything more about what the photo showed.

She saw tears break in her mama's eyes, accompanied by guttural sniffling from choked sinuses. Felissa's eyes welled up too, but she still felt the anger.

"Mama, what happened? You told me your papa was killed in an accident." The words came out in a shivering mass, falling to the ground like driving rain.

"Ma'am," started Lorman, breaking his self-imposed

silence. "If you know anything about this, I really want to find out, too."

Faith opened her mouth to speak, and then stopped. Felissa watched her, considering, weeping, fidgeting with her hands. All of a sudden she got up from her chair and started pacing around the room, idly running her fingers over the surfaces of the stove, refrigerator, counter and table.

"It's never easy to bring shame out into the open, Lissa." Faith grabbed a tissue and blew her nose into it, then continued. "I should have known better than to hide what happened from you. But I didn't think it mattered. Maybe I did, but I wanted to bury it, forever. Rest easy, Lorman, your grandpa didn't have anything to do with my papa's death.

"When your Granny Brown was dying, Lissa, I was with her every day in the hospital. Even when I wasn't on shift, I was there. One day, she had an old visitor. I didn't recognise him at all, but Granny Brown introduced him as Uncle John. She said he was my papa's brother. While they were talking, I heard him say, "I'm so sorry about Tom; you know, I still think about him a lot. I just hope for our children's sake there's more justice in this world than there was with those killers." When he was gone, I asked my mama about it. She was in a lot of pain, and the story she told me put her in even more discomfort, but she told me anyway.

"It was the early fifties, and my parents had been married for a few years. They lived with me in a one-bedroom apartment in the town. It was in a very poor neighbourhood. One day when I was about two-years-old, my mama was baking a pie and had it on the window sill to cool. It was a treat for my papa who didn't get a pie very often. With one thing and another, she got busy taking care of me and then looked back to the window and, what do you know, the pie was gone. In its place was a handkerchief. Dear me, your granny did cry when she told me the story.

"My papa got home from work and she showed him the handkerchief. They didn't know what to make of it and figured the pie had been stolen by some tramp. Next thing they knew, however, there was a loud knock on the door and it sounded like someone was trying to kick it in. My papa opened it, and there was this big white guy with his finger in my papa's chest. Three others were right behind him and stepped inside.

""You've been with my sister, mister, and no black is ever going to get away with that," the first man said.

"My papa told him: "I ain't been with your sister; I don't even know who you are. I'm married with a little girl right here.""

"Without missing a beat, he grabbed my papa by the arm and pointed to the kitchen table. "Never been with my sister, huh?" They saw the handkerchief sitting there. The men dragged him away with my mama and me screaming. The next day mama got word that he was dead. She didn't know what to do. She had hardly anyone to turn to. A couple took her in that already lived in one room. Mama got a job ironing laundry. I don't know how she survived the horror of it."

Felissa's world was being turned upside down. She glanced at Lorman as her mama paused.

"Who killed him?" asked Lorman. Felissa could feel the tension in his words and his anxiety to find out.

"That was the great shame of it, Lorman. Mama talked to the police, who said they would find the killers. They never caught anyone. They never did anything about it, either. Mama thought they might even have been there when he was killed. She said they were so patronising to her.

"One day a few weeks later, she was out delivering laundry

when a young white man asked her if she was Tom Brown's widow. It was Hank. He told her he knew her husband had been innocent. He went on to say that his brother, who he farmed with, told him about the lynching and had been involved. This brother, Billy Morton, had helped frame..." Here Faith's words faltered and she caught her breath as the tears came in torrents.

"H-he helped his friend, Bobby Jeffries, frame Granddad Brown because my papa had a job that Bobby wanted. It was nothing more than that. They stole the pie and put the hand-kerchief there. He got a man killed over a job. Not just any man, it was my PAPA. That man had no sister who'd been molested or raped or anything like that. The worst thing was that Bobby Jeffries was the son of the police chief. Billy Morton and Bobby skipped town, and Hank said his mother had received a brief phone call from Billy saying he was never coming back.

"My mama heard all this from Hank and was a bit sceptical, but he sounded sincere. He said he wanted to do something for her, because he felt responsible for what had happened since it was his brother who was involved.

"It turned out the couple mama was staying with knew Hank. They worked in a jam factory where he delivered blue-berries. He offered to let this couple and my mama live in a cottage on his farm, rent-free, and to give them the use of a farm truck. Though they were cautious at first, they accepted, since they were in such dire straits in the one-room apart-ment. As you know, your Granny Brown never remarried. The couple later moved out, and a few years after when I was still a little girl, Hank quietly subdivided the farm and gave the title to my mama. She raised chickens and blueberries until after I grew up and was married. She died not long after she told me the real story."

They were silent. Felissa sniffled. After a few minutes, Lorman looked up at Faith.

"What about the stuff in the shed? Do you know anything about that? Why would grandpa keep that stuff locked up in there? What about that...that thing painted on the door?"

"I don't know," Faith confessed. "There's a noose in there, and it's scary all right, but is it the same one? I have no idea who painted that thing on the door. That's a mystery to me, too. But you shouldn't have broken in there. You're going to have to tell your grandpa what you did. In the meantime, I'm not sure what to do. I was hoping to hear something back from the police."

"Mama," replied Felissa in a cracking voice. "The picture we found was of granddad strung up on a tree."

Felissa felt strange. Her insides felt all cramped and tight. She couldn't hold back the flood of hurt, shame and anger that was going through her. She got up and ran over to her mama and held her tight for a long time. Lorman looked on, a little embarrassed. Faith walked right up to him and put her arms around him, too, and he responded with a tight embrace.

Felissa was glad her mama had told her about this, but it felt like a betrayal, too. The truth had been hidden from her. In a way, she didn't blame her mama, but in another way she was angry about what she'd been told in the past. She wondered what Lorman felt about his grandfather. She was relieved that he wasn't implicated, but not too happy that it was Hank's brother that had killed her granddad.

After sorrowing together a little longer, they sat, letting the intense feelings ebb and flow. They talked some more while Faith made sandwiches to eat for lunch.

Suddenly Felissa realised they were all very jumpy. Every time a vehicle passed outside, she peeked through the front window. Her mama was just putting a couple of plates on the table when Felissa gave a shout.

"There's a red truck out there and it's pulling into Hank's farm."

****

Lorman looked out. An old truck was bouncing speedily into the drive that wound by Hank's house and through the farm. Lorman ran to look through the kitchen blinds.

Felissa heard her mama calling the police as she watched alongside Lorman. A white-haired man got out of the truck. He hauled a jerry can from the back of the vehicle and, to Felissa's horror, poured fuel onto Hank's veranda. He went back for another can and walked over to the shed, slopping gasoline against it, too. This must be Billy Morton, she thought. But where was Hank?

Suddenly Lorman rushed outside. Felissa was ready to scream. She watched as the white-haired man was coming back for a third can of fuel. In mid-stride, he saw Lorman and, quick as anything, pulled out a pistol. Lorman stopped short, about twenty feet away.

"Why the hell are you gonna set fire to this place?" Lorman yelled, ignoring the gun.

"Put your hands up or I'll blast your head off," roared the stranger. "Who the hell are you?" he continued.

"I'm related to you by blood and I don't want this farmhouse burnt down," Lorman spat back.

"You young whippersnapper! You don't know anything. This farm was taken away from me a long time ago. I didn't even know what had happened to it until recently. And what do I find out? Half the damn property is owned by a black woman. If it's the last thing I do, I'll make sure she can't have it, her and my betraying son-of-a-bitch brother." His words were fired in angry volleys, but then his tone changed to a slow, sarcastic drawl.

"I bet you're his grandson, aren't you? Probably the thing he loves most in this world. Well guess what, you're about to be tied up, my little man. You'll be under the sign of death that I put there last night. Yes sir. I wondered what that old fool Hank was doing up so late with the light on. I guess he was talking to you."

From the window, Felissa watched in horror as the old guy tied Lorman up with a coil of white rope.

"Are the police on their way?" she cried frantically to her mama, who nodded. They were riveted to the window, straining their ears for the first sound of a siren. Felissa wondered why the police hadn't been there all along if they knew the place was in danger, as Hank had said. And why, oh why, had Lorman run out there?

She saw her friend being led to the shed. The old guy kicked the door open with his boot, pushed Lorman inside and then emerged alone.

What happened next seemed to occur in slow motion. The white-haired guy took a book of matches from his pocket and pulled one out. He was going to light the house first. It occurred to Felissa that she couldn't hear Lorman screaming from inside the petrol-dowsed shed. Was he unconscious? All of a sudden there was a sound of sirens screaming in the distance. At almost the same moment, the old guy went to strike the match, but a projectile flew from the shed towards him and struck him full in the back of the head, knocking him over.

It was the crowbar.

Lorman emerged from the shed, carrying the rope, and hurried to tie up his Great Uncle Morton. Then three police cars screamed into the drive and half a dozen officers jumped out, pointing their guns at Lorman.

Faith and Felissa were already outside, making their way to Hank's property. Felissa screamed to the police that the truck belonged to the old guy on the ground and that Lorman was unarmed. He already had his hands up in the air.

Soon the weapons were lowered and Faith talked to an officer while a couple of others spoke to Lorman and then to the dazed old man who was starting to regain consciousness.

Shortly, a fire engine, sirens blaring, pulled up as well and, a few minutes later, Hank arrived in his old truck. The police spoke to him, and got him to identify his brother.

Felissa was so relieved that Lorman was okay. She and her mama both hugged him.

"I thought you were dead. You were all tied up and there was fuel everywhere. How did you escape?" asked Felissa, a smile of relief across her lips.

"I guess Great Uncle Billy forgot to make sure I wasn't holding my breath," answered Lorman. Felissa could see that he was still in shock, and it was just then that tears started flowing from his eyes.

****

That evening, after the fire fighters had cleaned up the fuel and the police had taken Hank's brother away, and when things had settled down somewhat, they all had a chance to talk together. Hank invited Faith and Felissa over for a barbecue.

Lorman still needed some answers.

"Grandpa, why were you gone all day?"

"Well now, Lorman, when I saw that paint job on the shed door this morning, I knew Billy had to be in town. I remembered from way back, him and his gang used it as a threat. I never told you about my brother, Billy, did I?"

Hank was talking almost without taking a breath. It was

all coming out now.

"We had this farm together, right where we're standing now. Billy, he wasn't the farming type, he was more of a rough-and-tumble rebel. He did his fair share some of the time, others not. Anyhow, one day I was out getting supplies and I came back and what do I find but a friend of Billy's named Bobby Jeffries in front of that shed, carrying a rifle. So I asked him what he was doing, and he says he's guarding "a nigger" for my brother Billy and I'd better not get in the way. So I left and drove away. I knew it was a delicate situation because Bobby's father was the chief of police in those days. I talked to another policeman I knew in town, and he assured me they'd send someone out. When I got back, Billy and Bobby were gone and so was their prisoner. I found out what happened to him later. Lynched. I was so disgusted. Billy and I fought, let me tell you. Violently. He was pretty scared, not only of me, but of what the law might do, despite Bobby's father and all. So after that the farm was mine.

"Then there was this morning. I went straight to the police station. I figured it was better to go in person than to phone. I made such a big mistake in not bringing you along. To think what I could have done to you! I just about got you killed." Hank pursed his lips, pained.

"I made another big mistake in town, and that was to mention that Billy was collaboratin' with Bobby Jeffries all those years ago. They wanted to know all about it, but I had a heck of a time convincing them because a lot of the old-timers remembered his father, old man Jeffries, when he was the police chief. I told them over and over again I needed some protection at the farm, but they wanted to find out for sure. I felt like I was being interrogated. They simply couldn't believe that a son of the police chief would do such a thing. Even when Faith called them the first time, they didn't do anything. They just kept on talking among themselves and then asked me more questions for half the morning. Finally, she called again when Billy showed up. What a miserable brother to have."

Lorman pondered that for a while. Then he looked at his grandpa again.

"In the shed, is that the noose that killed Tom Brown?"

"Yep, I believe so."

"Why'd you keep it?"

"To tell you the truth, Lorman, I didn't come across it until many years later, in fact just a couple of years ago. I was helping clean out a house in town, old Mrs. Martin's. She had died and I was helping her son. A floorboard in the attic was loose, so I pried it up before hammering it back into place. Underneath was this noose and the picture. At first I was horrified and wondered how it had got there, but then I realised the house had belonged to police chief Jeffries in the old days. His son Bobby must have hidden it there. I have no idea who took the picture. Mrs. Martin's son let me have them. All those years I tried to forget what had happened, but then I didn't want to forget. Though I didn't exactly know what to do with them. I sort of had the idea of getting the shed shipped off somewhere and making a kind of memorial out of it. To show what pathetic prejudice, misused power and the miscarriage of justice does to people. Instead I just planted roses, but it played on my mind.

"If you remember anything, Lorman, remember that if you don't understand someone, talk to them. Get to know them. You might be taking a chance but, for me, it's a risk I'd be willing to take, be they American, Asian, African, European or even Australian for that matter."

Lorman cracked a smile, but he was still puzzled by one thing.

"Why didn't you tell me about this after you found that stuff?"

"You know, I think it was because I was afraid, Lorman. I was ashamed of my brother and I didn't know what you'd think of me. Shame can be a powerful thing and it can lead to family secrets kept for years. I was wrong not to tell you. Here I am, seventy-five, and I still have a lot to learn. So do you, though, buster. Don't go running up to anyone with a loaded gun again anytime soon, okay?"

"You got it, grandpa."

****

Felissa and her mama walked across the lawn after the barbecue, making their way past the barn and along the house. They stopped under Felissa's bedroom window. It was late twilight and the air was completely still, as if they were standing inside a postcard, the moment captured. The fragrant scent of red roses wafted into their senses.

"Granddad liked red roses, didn't he, mama?"

"How did you know that?"

"You've always had them planted here and taken care of them better than anything else on the farm, even the blueberries. Plus, Hank has red roses planted around the shed. He put them in a couple of years ago. I have a feeling he found that out from Granny Brown."

"Girl, you are so right. That was what she told me about him. He loved red roses, especially the ones that smelled really good.

"I was thinking, honey. I'm sorry I didn't share this pain with you before. In fact, I lied about it because I was ashamed of what had happened in our family. I guess I never should have been so ashamed. He was a good person, but something terrible happened to him. That doesn't mean we should forget him. I remember him whenever I look at these roses. I remember the stories Granny Brown told me. You should be able to remember, too. I'm sorry, honey. Please forgive me. Parents aren't perfect.

"I do," her daughter whispered. "Neither are daughters."

Together they watched the last glow of light sink away.

Thursday

By
Joel Willans

The alarm drills into my dream, trying to suck me away from an female aerobics class. Miranda is using a PowerPoint presentation to explain why my star jumps are wrong. Sadie, displaying her sumptuous breasts in a very low cut t-shirt, is shouting at me to work it. It's a strange combination and I can't think what's caused the two to be united by my imagination.

I lean over and slap my alarm clock, wondering if my unconscious is showcasing some latent sexual fantasy or just warning me about my lack of fitness. Nuzzling my pillow, I focus my energies on returning to the company of the ladies, but reality is too stubborn. My waking mind starts to nag.

"You can't be late this morning," it says.

"You have a very important meeting."

"You know she's looking for the chance to sack you."

These thoughts always sound like my mother. I can't handle it any longer so I open my eyes. Light, like that from a bulb stuffed in a grey sock, slices through a gap in the curtains. I unravel myself from the warm embrace of my quilt and stumble to the bathroom. I study myself in the mirror. I look like shit. My eyes are meant to be my best feature, big and brown, but now they're nothing more than dark slits cupped in shadow. I pout at myself like a porn star. Sadie used to say I had kissable lips, but then she had a talent for talking bollocks.

I run my hand over my head, enjoying the soft prickles of my shaved hair. I have it as a number two because it's easy to deal with. There is no messing around with gel or wax or blow-drying. I have estimated that this gives me at least ten extra minutes in bed every single working day.

I start to shave. Normally on a Thursday I'd leave it, but today I have to go and see Zoom, one of our major client's ad agency. They have been shafting me for about three months, putting all their money into our main rival, *Car Lovers Weekly*. Miranda is coming, too, as she's looking for an excuse to get rid of me. I smear the foam over my face. When I was a kid, I used to love doing this. Using the back of my dad's razor, I'd scrape the soapy cream off, marvelling at the way my face reappeared in shiny pink strips. I couldn't wait until I could do it for real. Now, if I had a choice, I'd never bother.

I'm determined to look my best, so I put a lot of effort into my facial hair. My half-hearted goatee beard takes quite a bit of work. It's not full-on, more of an Errol Flynn 'tache with a bit at the bottom. I'd love to go for something more flamboyant, maybe a combination of Salvador Dali and a Spitfire pilot. Unfortunately, when you're an advertising salesman, you don't have the same leeway with facial hair as mad artists and wartime daredevils. Even now I get grief.

"Oie, Parksie, you missed a bit."

"Why do you have a toothbrush on your chin?"

"Do you have to feed that?"

This is nothing unusual. In the world of media sales, constant abuse is as close to civilised conversation as it gets.

Once I'm done in the bathroom, I rummage through my wardrobe. I pick out my sharpest and most expensive suit, single-breasted, black with a slight retro feel, a black shirt, fat silver cufflinks and a nearly black tie from Kenzo that cost seventy quid. I know this as Sadie left the price tag on when she gave it to me for Christmas. Fashion is an essential component to the success of any advertising salesperson. "It's imperative that you are more stylish than your client," Miranda always says. "If you turn up wearing a tie worth more than their entire wardrobe, it screws them up completely." Today, more than any other day, I need to do exactly that.

I've got twenty minutes to catch the train. The walk is ten. Normally, I'd lounge around until the last minute, but this morning I can't take any chances. Miranda has a fetish about lateness that borders on psychotic. I make do with a piece of toast and a swig of orange juice, then hit the road.

The sky is the colour of a battleship. It feels as if the sun can't be bothered. People march with their heads down past the terraced growth of houses that cramp the street. Cars squat in the road, spewing fumes and beeping like angry robots. Even though I work on the country's most widely read car magazine, I hate these machines. It's the way they divide people into two subsets, drivers and walkers. You rarely come across a mouthy, arrogant walker, but give someone wheels and they fancy themselves as invincible – Gods encased in metal bubbles.

After one deep breath, I take my first step into Thursday's world. I smile to myself as I walk past the jammed traffic, stationary Audis, Volvos and Fords wedged as tight as tins on a supermarket shelf. To celebrate this little victory, I spark up a Marlboro Light. The smoke floods my lungs and gives me the faintest of rushes. I am not a big smoker. I treat each cigarette like a fine Havana cigar hand-rolled by Cuban virgins. That is, of course, unless I'm binge-drinking pints, in which case I can go through a pack of twenty in about five minutes.

The station sucks in a frothing mass of people, like a giant vacuum cleaner. Everyone wears frowns that crease their features into hard, sharp lines. I bundle my way down the stairs, swinging my bag to clear a path. The platform clock tells me I'm seven minutes early. I relax a little, but I take nothing for granted. I've no doubt that getting to work is the most hardcore sport the twenty-first century has to offer. To be a successful player, you need both luck and the ability to disengage totally from your fellow human. I have neither.

"The 8.24 service to London Waterloo will be delayed by approximately thirteen minutes. Southwest Trains apologises for any inconvenience this may cause," an unapologetic female voice announces.

People in the crowd shuffle their morning papers, stamp a foot or tut, others swear under their breath. That's the sum total of their annoyance. I feel like punching someone, but instead I steam towards the ticket office.

"Give me a complaint form!"

"What's the other word?" a woman with a tight bun and square glasses says.

"I'm not in the mood for manners right now. Just give me a complaint form. In fact, give me ten."

She sighs and counts out ten pieces of paper. I take them with a flourish and return to my spot near the edge of the platform. I feel better for about thirty seconds. One of the reasons why I despise Southwest Trains is that they give me no outlet for my anger, except a stuck-up woman in a plastic box.

If the tube is running okay, I should still be all right. For the next twelve minutes I am mesmerised by the clacking of fat, yellow numerals on the station clock. It's a strangely calming sound and I start to feel all Zen about the situation. However, my budding inner peace is shredded when the train chugs into the station. It's so full of people it looks like an attempt at a Guinness World Record.

The doors slide open and people bulge out. The platform crowd barges forward, attracted to the bodies on the train like iron filings to a magnet. I throw my weight into the scrum. Someone jabs me in the back with an umbrella. I unleash an elbow and hear a grunt. I lunge forward and fling my body through the decreasing gap.

My face is squashed against someone's shoulder and the edge of my suit is pinched between the two doors, but I'm in. I once read that you could fit the entire population of the planet on the Isle of Wight, if only they all stood up straight and didn't move. This is what it's like in my carriage. I wiggle a bit to create a few extra inches of personal space. At the end of the aisle, I spot a pinstriped wide boy with acres of room, reading the *Financial Times*.

I can't stand 'City boys'. It disgusts me how they earn massive pay cheques by doing nothing more than making rich people richer. I know I'm not in the most morally sound industry myself, but what choice do you have when you leave university with a useless degree and a huge debt? You take the first job you get. Media sales is easy to get into but hard to get out of. To start with, there's the amazing buzz you get when you close a deal. You become addicted to people saying yes. Then there's the perks – the promise of fat commission cheques, an expenses account, visits to swanky restaurants, corporate jollies to exotic locations, your own laptop and the latest mobile phone. At first, after three years of university poverty, it's as if you've died and gone to heaven. It's not like that anymore, though. Now it feels like a golden chain weighing me down.

The air on the train is a blend of aftershave and fruity perfume, sweat and stale cigarette smoke. The only other time I get this close to strangers is when I go clubbing. Clubbers, though, are celebrating their humanity, while on the train people are denying it. It's an amazing skill, to be able to hold your emotions in suspended animation and to completely ignore other people, despite being no more than five centimetres from them.

When I get off at Vauxhall, I only have thirty-one minutes left to get to work. I break into a run, swearing at people who get in my way. I eyeball old women shuffling like shackled prisoners, glammed up secretaries tottering on their heels, and the armies of suited blokes blocking my path. I rush down the steps into the underground. It smells of piss and old beer. The harsh light bleaches faces, making everyone look ill. I glide down the escalator, past adverts for West End shows, makeup and mobile phones.

As the crowd splits into two streams, one going north and one south, I spot Skinner. This is both a curse and a blessing. It means that if I'm late, he will be late too. It also means he might spot me and I'd have to talk to him. I pull out yesterday's *Evening Standard* from my bag and pretend to read it as I walk to the end of the platform. Skinner is nowhere in sight. I'd have heard him if he'd seen me. He has a voice like a tannoy system.

The tube bursts from the tunnel and shoots past me, a thousand different faces flashing past my eyes. Every space is crammed. I grit my teeth and get ready. I find myself between two doors. Scanning the crowd, I go for the entrance where there's more women than men. As I burrow into the throng, a girl with a pierced lip asks me what I'm doing. I heave past her. She tries to turn but I nudge her to the side, flinging out both arms as I barge my way in. The hard stares I provoke drain me.

The disapproval of other passengers fills the air like a cloud of smoke. I try not to care what they think. It's survival of the fittest, a gladiatorial contest, eat or be eaten. I'm still thinking this when I catch the look of a beautiful girl with baby deer eyes. She shakes her head at me and looks at the floor. My cheeks go hot. It feels as if an angel has told me off. I want to say that I'm actually not a bad bloke, but of course I don't.

As we crawl through the earth, my embarrassment slowly transforms into bubbling anger. It's all Miranda's fault. She's the one who makes me act like this. Now the beautiful girl thinks I'm an obnoxious prick. Does it really matter if I'm not exactly on time? It's not my problem if the trains are always late. By the time the tube gets to Oxford Circus, my hands are fists and I'm frothing with rage. I decide to take it out on Miranda the only way I can, by not rushing. I walk up the steps and rejoin the outside world. The street is churning with people, buses and taxis all regimented by seconds, minutes and hours.

I amble to the office, noticing things I've never seen before. The elaborate design of the gables along Carnaby Street, the perfect choreography of pigeons as they bob their heads together, the smell of oven-fresh baguettes. I don't know how long this stroll takes me, but when I arrive at my desk, Skinner is already sat at his. He looks at his watch.

"Afternoon," he says. "Do you have a late gene?"

"I don't know; I haven't checked."

"Well, perhaps you should."

"Since when has my biological make-up been anything to do with you?"

"I was just trying to find a scientific explanation for you never being on time."

"Maybe you should focus on finding a scientific explanation for your oversized head."

This shuts him up. Skinner is very sensitive about the size of his forehead. It's his Achilles's heel. I'm just starting to feel better about the morning when I see Miranda striding towards me with a stare that could melt an iceberg. She looks like she's just stepped off a catwalk. Her hair is all done up in ringlets and she's wearing shiny knee-high boots with dangerously pointed toes. I sit up straight and stick my chest out, even though this gesture feels as pointless as shaving before facing a firing squad.

"Are you on flexi-time?" she asks.

"Sorry, Southwest trains were screwed up."

"They're always screwed up. Why don't you get up earlier?"

"If I got up any earlier, it wouldn't be worth going to bed."

She doesn't smile. "This is not a game, Duncan. You need to take your work more seriously. Otherwise you'll soon have no reason to get up at all."

I nod. I'm tired of her threatening me.

"I expect you to be ready to go by eleven," she says.

"But the meeting's not until half past."

"One," she says, holding up a finger capped with a blood-red nail, "I am never late. Two, arriving early is a sign of professionalism. That's something you should've learnt by now."

Seemingly satisfied, she walks away. I'm glad to have her out of my face. Miranda is a nightmare. First of all, she's utterly unpredictable. On my first day at the company, she took our team out for lunchtime beers. I thought we'd bonded. She was laughing at my gags and I even got a sneaky suspicion she was giving me the eye. The next morning she told me to get coffees for everyone.

"I'm a sales professional, not a delivery boy," I said.

"I don't care. While I pay your wages, you'll do what I say," she said.

"You haven't paid me anything yet. I've only been here for two days."

This got a laugh from everyone. Miranda stood up and, with a frozen smile, ordered me into her office.

"Don't you ever speak to me like that in front of my team!" she shouted, her face inches from mine. "You are a nobody here until you prove yourself. Now get out of my sight."

The unpredictability of Miranda's mood swings is partly due to her cocaine habit. If she's been out on a big night during the week, I make it my business to avoid her the next day. She's also difficult to work for because she wants everyone to lust after her. She knows I don't, and I think this is why she wants me out. The irony is that if I hadn't been going out with Sadie at the time, I'd probably have said yes to her drunken advance. Before Miranda became bitter and spiteful towards me, I thought her blend of dominating personality and physical fitness was sexy. Now it just annoys me. She uses it to pull the strings of her mainly male sales team, like an expert puppeteer. Four-hundred years ago she might've been burnt as a witch.

Skinner leans forward, a smirk decorating his face. He reminds me of the Joker out of '*Batman*'. "Oh dear, oh dear. You're going to be in all sorts of trouble today."

"Really? And how do you know that, Sherlock?"

"She was out on a bender last night. Gidders saw her in Blue Lounge, then in the Doghouse. He left at one and she was still buying rounds."

"Nothing I can't handle."

"Don't worry. She might not bin you, just move you to classified. I'm sure the second-hand car dealers in East Ham will love you."

I need a fag break so I tramp back through the office. It's open plan and decorated with primary colours. Harsh neon light reflects off the glass walls of the meeting rooms. The windows are like the slits used by bowmen in castles. I've always assumed this combination is a result of some theory in interior design. Maybe it's meant to increase productivity. If so, it doesn't work for me. It feels as if I spend my day on the set of a Saturday morning children's television show. When I get out into the street, Gidders is already there.

"Alright mate, how's it going?" he says.

"Very badly. I'm going with Miranda to a meeting with Zoom."

"Nightmare. Who looks after the account?"

"Giles Harcourt."

"Oh, that annoying twat. Isn't he shagging that girl from *Car Lovers Weekly*?"

"Which one?"

"I don't remember her name, but I saw them getting it together at the last awards party."

I can't believe it. The award ceremony was just before Miranda gave me the account. She must've known it would go pear-shaped. Now if I don't turn this around, she'll get shot of me. This is my last chance. I know it's only a job, but my whole life revolves around my monthly pay cheque. I've got used to the injection of cash and the stuff I can buy with it. You can't do anything in London without money. You might as well not exist.

I study a boy hunched up on a bit of cardboard on the pavement opposite. Wrapped in a dirty mound of blankets, he stares blankly with his thrust out hand sign-posting his desperation. Nobody stops. Nobody even looks at him. Penniless, he is invisible.

When I was a kid, people used to ask me what I wanted to be when I grew up. At first I never knew, but when I was about ten I started to say I wanted to be a millionaire. As I got a bit older, I refined this statement. I wanted to be a millionaire by the time I was twenty-one. I'm now twenty-seven and not even close. It doesn't bother me, though, as I've realised it wasn't the money I was after. It was the freedom to do what I wanted. Unfortunately, I'm not close to that either.

"You coming back in?" Gidders asks.

I nod, suddenly feeling very hollow, as if my bones have been sucked out. I follow him back to the office and watch him slump into his seat. Gidders wanted to be a rock star. His voice is amazing and he was even on telly a couple of times when he was younger. Then his group got a manager who wanted to turn them into a boy-band. They weren't having any of it, so now they just play pubs at weekends. Gidders says he's glad, but I'm not so sure. I think it's sad to see him on the phone when he could've been on stage. I wonder if someone will look at me in a few years and think it's sad I'm still making the same calls.

"Miranda rang," Skinner says as I sit back down. "She didn't sound very pleased."

"What, can't a man go for a piss without being hassled?"

"She thought you'd gone for a sneaky ciggy."

"I wonder what would make her think that."

"You tell me."

I start to get my stuff together for the meeting. When my bag is packed with circulation certificates, media packs, old issues of *Smart Car World*, my phone, my laptop and my business cards, I make my way to Miranda. She's on the phone and gestures at me to sit down. I listen to her shouting at someone, thinking it must be something to do with work. Then she puts down the phone after saying goodbye to her mum.

"Got everything?"

"Yeah, everything."

"Show me."

"What?"

"Show me!"

I empty the bag and watch her scour the contents.

"Where are the other car magazines?"

"I don't sell on those."

"They're part of our portfolio," she says, slapping one of each onto the desk. "I'll meet you outside in five, I have to nip to the ladies."

In my experience these five minutes could mean anything up to half-an-hour, so once outside I spark another cigarette. As I draw the smoke into my body, I watch people steaming past me. I love observing and Soho's brilliant for that. It mixes villains with film directors, prostitutes with stallholders, beggars with marketing managers. It's almost as if someone's purposely built a place to attract the most diverse range of people possible. I don't think there's anywhere else in London I'd want to work. This thought depresses me and makes me even more desperate to win back the client's business.

"I don't see a cab." Miranda says, strutting down the steps.

"I thought we could walk," I answer.

"Have you seen the heels on these boots?"

One of the new black cabs drives towards us. It reminds me of a giant, bloated beetle. I stick out my arm and thank my lucky stars when the car slows to a halt.

"Where to, gov?" the cabbie asks.

"Top of Tottenham Court Road."

"Don't you know the address?" Miranda asks.

"Not off the top of my head. I normally go on foot, so I don't need the address."

"How environmentally sound of you." As she leans back in the seat, the leather squeaks like a kitten stroked the wrong way.

I don't bother replying. Miranda's contempt for me is almost as suffocating as her perfume. As we crawl through the tiny streets, I wonder what would've happened if I'd followed her outside when she'd asked me to. It was at Gidders' birthday party downstairs at the Slug and Lettuce, a huge wooden space that always makes me think of a vast sauna. Miranda had her credit card behind the bar, an entirely false act of generosity as she'd claim it all back on expenses later. I'd been necking champagne and then beer, a combination that always screws me up. I was staggering back from the cigarette machine when Miranda swanned up to me like a princess at a palace ball.

"What you up to, Duncan?"

"Just buying fags."

"That's just what I need."

I pulled open the packet and handed her one.

"Light?"

I flicked open my lighter. She wrapped her hands around mine and I noticed her pupils were the size of chocolate buttons.

"Do you have a girlfriend?" she asked.

"Yeah."

"Living together?"

"Not yet."

"How old is she?"

"A couple of years younger."

"You're not into more experienced women, then?" She let the question hang in the air, tilted her head and blew a stream of smoke into my face. I considered my answer carefully, wondering if she was trying to make me squirm. The drink puffed me up with confidence.

"I've yet to have the pleasure."

"Well, if you follow me outside, tonight might be your lucky night," she said and then strode up the stairs to the exit.

I stood there staring up at the door, wondering what it would be like to get intimate with Miranda. Twice I started towards the exit, twice I stopped and came back. The furthest I got was the third step. It wasn't only the thought of Sadie, who was already beginning to show signs of irrational jealousy, but also the consequences of getting it on with my boss. If I'm completely honest, it was raw fear.

"Recognise anything yet?" Miranda says, clicking her fingers.

"The next left please, mate."

The cabbie spins the wheel round in his meaty hands. We pull up in front of a tall Georgian town house with the word 'Zoom' emblazoned across its entrance. The sign looks out of place, as though someone has sprayed graffiti on a church wall. Miranda leaves me to pay. She straightens her hair and walks up the steps. I follow her into the reception, catching the door that she lets swing back into my face.

"Miranda Good," she says to a pretty girl behind the reception desk. "I've got a meeting with Giles Harcourt."

"What company, please?"

Miranda looks as if she's just been asked her weight.

"IDX," she says.

"I'll let him know. Take a seat, please." She points to an orange sofa that wouldn't look out of place on Blue Peter.

I plonk myself down. The person who did our office seems to have got their hands on their reception, too. It feels as if I'm sitting in a rainbow. The walls are littered with adverts and framed certificates heralding the creative genius of the agency. A table football game stands next to the sofa. The coffee counter is a cloud-shaped fish tank with a glass cover.

These are exactly the type of furnishings that advertising agencies dazzle their clients with. The sad thing is that it works. The first time I ever went into an agency reception, I was blown away. I couldn't believe how cool it was. It felt more like the chill-out room of a club than an office. I remember thinking how lucky I was to work in such an exciting industry. This feeling lasted almost a year. It was Sadie who first suggested that advertising might not be as glamorous as I had thought.

"It's all bullshit. They are peddling lies. It's a façade," she said one night.

"What do you mean?"

"They've turned deception into an art form. There's nothing to celebrate about getting people to buy stuff they don't need."

"That's bollocks. They're promoting people's products in an inventive way, that's all."

"God, sometimes you're so naive. There are children in my class who are more clued-up than you."

Sadie always said that sort of thing when she wanted to wind me up. She taught history at a comprehensive in Lewisham. I'd never seen her in action, but I have no doubt she peppered her lessons with socialist rhetoric, which is ironic when you consider she's a product of the public school system. When I think about it, it's strange that I ever went out with her. I've always hated public school-kids.

It started off with my cousin who went to a public school almost next door to my primary school. One day when he'd stayed over, mum asked me to walk with him to his classes. We were hounded for the entire journey. Even my friends threw stones at me for hanging out with a 'snob'. In the end, I made him walk on the other side of the road. This was my first experience of the us-and-them-mentality promoted by the public school system.

Giles Harcourt is a perfect example of this, which is one of the many reasons he gets on my nerves.

"Hi guys. Thanks for coming over," he says, emerging on cue from a pink, fluffy door. He's wearing combat trousers and a t-shirt with the word 'Talent' splashed across the chest. I feel completely overdressed. He flashes a perfect smile and flicks his hair out of his eyes.

Miranda stands up to present her cheek, which Giles dutifully air-kisses. I reach out my hand.

"How's it going, fella?" he says.

"Brilliantly," I say.

"Great. I've booked Jackson Pollock for us."

"Sorry?"

"The Jackson Pollock room." He laughs, sounding like an excited pig. "Our meeting rooms are all named after the twentieth century's greatest creators. There's the John Lennon, the

Andy Warhol, the Virginia Woolf…"

"Very clever," Miranda says.

"Inspired," I say.

"Inspiration is our business, fella."

The Jackson Pollock room is, as you would expect, spotted. Even as I sit down, I feel a headache coming on. I can't imagine a place more likely to cause migraines. Miranda takes a chair at the head of the table; I place myself between her and Giles. His cologne smells of marzipan. I notice he hasn't shaved.

"So, what's happening with your client?" I say and pull out my laptop.

"Oh please, not another PowerPoint," he says. "If I have to sit through another slideshow this week, I will lose it."

"It'd help me show you how our readership compares with your client's target group."

"I know everything there is to know about your magazine's readership."

"Well, then you'll know it has a greater percentage of 'AB1' males than any other car magazine." I glance at Miranda, expecting her to lend some support. She says nothing.

"Listen, fella. Who was it that said statistics are nothing more than lies and damned lies?"

"We spend hundreds of thousands of pounds on our circulation."

"I'm sure you do, but I rely on gut feeling. It says that *Car Lovers Weekly* provides the best vehicle for my client to reach their core audience."

From the corner of my eye, I can see Miranda shaking her head. My career is slowly but surely going down the pan. I've appealed to Giles's logic and been slapped down. I decide to play my joker.

"Perhaps we could discuss your client's contingency budget

over lunch?"

"Where do you have in mind?"

"How does Jezzo's sound?"

"Right on, fella. There might be a tad left in the pot for special deals. I'll just pop upstairs and grab my jacket."

I watch amazed at the speed at which he leaves the room.

"Brilliant. A textbook example of how to not to overcome an objection," Miranda says.

"I had no choice."

"What do you mean you had no choice? Perhaps you could've tried selling some of the benefits of the magazine."

"You know his girlfriend works for *Car Lovers Weekly*."

"Don't give me excuses. You've already had a warning about your attitude. You have to get them back into the magazine, it's as simple as that."

"He says there might be something left in the pot."

"Let's hope so for your sake."

I sit there in silence, fighting an urge to tell Miranda to stick the job. I've always had a love/hate relationship with my work. I like meeting new people, I like working in Soho and I like the cash I get, but is that really enough? I certainly don't want to be doing this forever. The problem is, there's nothing for me to do instead. I'm drifting through life without purpose and the only thing that anchors me is work. If I do leave, I want it to be on my own terms, in a blaze of glory. I want people to say what a shame it was that Duncan Parks decided to move on, as he was such a sound bloke. Probably, like everyone else on the planet, I just want to be liked.

Of course I dream of doing other things with my life, but they seem as likely to happen to me as landing on the moon. I've only ever talked about this to Sadie. Once, after I'd been ranting about work again, she asked me what I'd do if I could be anything in the world.

"A photographer," I said.

"But you haven't even got a camera."

"I thought this was a hypothetical question."

"Okay, what sort of photographer?"

"I'd work for magazines like *National Geographic*, travelling to take pictures of the world's most amazing things."

"Like what?"

"Everything. People, places, animals...there's so much beauty on this planet that deserves to be immortalised."

She reached over and touched my face. "That's such a wonderful thing to say. I didn't know you had it in you."

That night we had the best sex we'd had for ages. Three weeks later I found out she'd been shagging the new PE Teacher at her school.

Giles bounces back into the room. He's wearing a parka coat with a massive furry hood. It makes him look like a cross between a Brit pop guitarist and an arctic explorer.

"Have you called to book a table, fella?"

"Good point," I say.

I pull out my mobile, making sure Giles gets an eyeful. It has a still and a video camera, internet browsing, an interactive map, a radio and, more importantly, a wide selection of games. I flick through my address book.

"You don't happen to have their number, do you?" I ask him.

"Hang on, I'll just check." He pulls out a slither of metal that looks like a silver playing card, holds it to his mouth and says Jezzo.

The silver playing card emits a call tone. I cringe as Giles asks for a table in the pricey downstairs restaurant rather than in the cheaper upstairs brasserie.

"Job done," he says. He sees me staring at his mobile. "Slick hey, fella? Got it in Japan. Don't know how I survived without it before. It's got a broadband connection, an MP3 player…"

"I'm hungry. Can you continue this in the cab?" Miranda says.

For the first time all day, I'm pleased she has accompanied me.

"Yeah, of course. You know what us boys are like, crazy for our toys," Giles says, giving me a nudge.

"Can't get enough of them," I say.

We trail Miranda out. As soon as I leave Jackson Pollock, I begin to feel better. The walls had provoked an unpleasant memory of the cards they show at school to test you for colour blindness, lots of spots splattered together to make up a number. My problem's always been green and brown, both look the same to me. The school nurse called my mum in when they discovered it. I think that's the first time she was disappointed in me.

"What number is this, Duncan?" the nurse had said, holding up the dotted card.

"I can't see one."

"It's a seven," mum said, pointing.

"Where?"

"Use your eyes! It's as clear as day."

"I can't see a seven."

"There!" mum shouted.

"It's just loads of dots."

The nurse explained that colour blindness was very common among boys and that there was no reason to worry. Mum nodded, but she said nothing to me on the way home. I think she saw it as a failure and maybe blamed herself. It was the first of many, and she seemed to take each as a personal affront. Getting the sack will just be another to add to the ever-growing list.

We squeeze into another cab. Miranda and Giles take the big seat and I'm left to perch on the little flip-down stool. I wonder what the cabbie would say if you asked him to guess what industry we work in. Giles looks like a posh student, Miranda could be mistaken for a fashion editor and me, I probably look like a foppish gangster. I imagine he'd think I was taking the piss if I told him we're all in the business of flogging cars.

Miranda's throwing the names of exotic holiday locations around like confetti. Giles is congratulating her on being such an adventurer while dropping in his own experiences of far-away places. I'd bet my next commission cheque that even if these two went away to a jungle in Borneo, or a desert in Uzbekistan, they'd find a five-star Sheraton to stay in. I stifle a yawn. I can't think of two people I'd less like to have lunch with.

"Where are you jetting off to next, fella?"

"Blackpool," I say. "I can't get enough of the lights."

"Oh, right. Cool. You're doing the northern thing?"

"Yeah, I go every year. I don't know what it is about the place that just keeps drawing me back. It just has this magical quality."

Miranda is puckering her face at me, so I shut up. She knows that last year I went to Thailand and not Blackpool, because she was the one who gave me the time off. Giles is scratching his head. He seems lost for words. This makes me feel happier than I've felt all morning.

The cab creaks to a halt. Miranda and Giles walk into the restaurant while I get a receipt from the driver. He asks me if I want it left blank, and I thank him but say no. His shock at this little act of honesty would be considerably less if he knew I've got an entire book of stolen receipts in my bedside drawer.

I walk into Jezzo's. It's all glass, big lights, gold furnishings and noise. Miranda and Giles have already been taken to the table, so I wander over.

"Can I help you, sir?" a waiter says in a voice that makes him sound like he is gay, but trying to be French.

"I'm with them," I say.

He raises two perfectly plucked eyebrows. "Oh, I see. I thought sir and madam were a couple. Please take a seat, I'll be with you in a moment."

Miranda and Giles don't even bother to acknowledge my arrival. This, even more than the remarks of the wannabe Frenchman, makes me feel like an unwanted accessory to the lunch. I check out the menu. As this may be my last meal on the company, I decide to throw caution to the wind and go for the most expensive dishes on offer. The trouble is, like most of the restaurants in Soho, Jezzo's endorses the law of diminishing returns. The more you pay, the less food you get. Taken to its logical extremes, if I were to pay a thousand quid for a starter, I'd be served a crumb on a plate the size of a satellite dish.

"What do you fancy, fella?"

"I'm going for the duck liver with white truffle compote as a starter and the elderberry-marinated veal for main."

Miranda shoots a glare at me over the top of her menu.

"What are we drinking? Red or white?" I ask.

"May I recommend the Chateauneuf du Pape and the Chablis," the waiter says, having silently appeared at my shoulder.

I check his recommendations and see they're the two priciest bottles on the menu.

"Any preference?"

"Well, both are very good on the palate, though I'm normally into a lighter bouquet myself," Giles says.

Miranda shrugs. "I don't care. I won't be drinking much anyway."

We both know this is a lie, but it's her only opportunity to register disapproval at my behaviour. Giles, on the other hand, has a toothpaste advert smile splitting his face. He knows he's being lavished and is loving it. I wait until they've ordered their food and then bring up business.

"So, you were saying there might have a bit tucked away for special deals."

"To be honest with you, fella, it'd have to be real special."

"We've got a luxury car supplement coming up next month and, between you and me, I suspect they'll be getting some very good editorial coverage."

"I should hope so. They're one of the world's leading car brands."

"Which is exactly why they should be in one of the world's leading car magazines."

"They are – *Car Lovers Weekly.*"

I look at Miranda. She's leaning back in her chair, arms crossed.

"You and I both know that in terms of reputation, circulation and editorial coverage, it can't compare to our magazine," I say.

"All good things come to an end."

"What does that mean?"

"Complacency, fella. When you've been the market-leader for a while, standards start to slip."

"What on earth are you talking about?" Miranda says, unable to take this dissing of our magazine any longer.

"I'm saying that you shouldn't take people's business for granted, that's all."

"We never take anything for granted," I say. "Listen, if I put together an attractive package for the next issue, would you be interested?"

"Can't guarantee it, fella, but I'll have a look."

The discussion comes to an end when the waiter asks me if I want to taste the wine. I say yes, but what I'd really like to do is pour it over Giles' head. I appear to be lavishing a large chunk of my expenses on him in return for his promise to have a look. I know that's not good enough and so does Miranda. By just having a look, Giles might as well have doffed a black cap and condemned my career at the company to death.

I would never have guessed they'd be such a pain. Miranda gave me their account the day after Gidders' birthday. I don't know how long she waited outside for me that night because I said my goodbyes and sneaked out the other way. I didn't want to go into work the next day. I hoped she might have forgotten about our conversation, but realised that was probably wishful thinking. I'd been at my desk for about five minutes when she called me into her office. I fully expected her to go mental, but instead she told me she'd decided to give me a new account. I couldn't believe my luck. I tried to call Sadie, but she was at lunch, so I called my dad instead.

"Brilliant, can you sort me a new car out then?" he said.

"Sort what out?"

"Maybe a cheap BM, I'd love one of those new 320s."

"And how exactly am I meant to do that?"

"Just give them a free ad or something."

"It doesn't quite work that way, dad."

He got moody after that, said what's the point of me working for a car magazine if I can't get discounted cars. He has always loved BMWs. When I was a kid, he bought a big family one. Then, as I got older, they gradually got smaller and faster. When my parents got divorced, he got a black soft-top two-seater with a leather interior and tinted windows. I told him people would think he was a drug dealer, but he just sniffed and said I was jealous.

This highlights how little he really knows me. I'd never get jealous about a car. It also shows how different we are. He loves cars, I hate them. He also thinks selling ads is a complete waste of my degree, which of course it is. However, his alternative, which he has pitched to me ever since I was old enough to listen, is in my opinion equally pointless. He wants me to join the army. His rationale for this is that three generations of Parks have served in Her Majesty's forces and that it would make a man of me. The history thing I can handle, but I've never been happy with the second reason. It basically implies I'm not masculine enough for his liking.

If he could see me now, burying my nose in a wine glass and making appreciative noises, his worst fears might just be confirmed. I take a swig of the thick red liquid. It's nice and fruity with a slight peppery taste. I know nothing about wines, so I'm not sure if this is how it's meant to taste, but I tell the waiter it's fine. He gives me a look that says I know you're a fraud. He must be used to that. At lunchtime, this place is full of suits on corporate lunches, living it up on other people's cash. I watch as he fills Miranda's glass. She makes no effort to stop him.

"Thanks, fella," Giles says once his glass is full.

"Joel," the waiter says.

"Sorry, fella?"

"My name's Joel."

"Oh, right, nice one. I always thought that was a French girl's name."

"It's unisex."

"Lucky you," Giles says and winks.

The waiter looks confused and asks whether we're ready to order. I stick with my original choice. Giles goes for the same starter and a carpaccio while Miranda, telling us she's got to look after her figure, has a rocket salad followed by baby chicken. Giles says her figure must be a pleasure to look after, which earns him a big smile. I make a toast to put an end to the sickening compliments. Giles downs half his glass in one and excuses himself to go to the gents.

"So far, so bad," Miranda immediately puts in.

"He says he's willing to have a look at a proposal."

"We both know what that means."

"You have to give me a chance to put something on paper for him."

"You've had plenty of chances. If you'd taken them when they were offered, things might be different."

I really can't get my head around her. I can't be the first-ever person to blow her out. I wonder if she goes out of her way to destroy the life of everyone who says no. If I were that sensitive, destroying lives would be my full-time job. What annoys me most about this whole revenge thing, besides the outrageous overreaction and pettiness, is that I'm actually quite a good salesperson. I've never been brilliant – if there was a '*Top Gun*' sales academy I wouldn't make it, but neither would I be in the dunces' class. Most of my clients like me. I used to have a good market share against my competitors and I've made the company a decent amount of cash. I was nicely drifting along, but then gradually, after that night, my targets started getting harder, I was given problem accounts and told to use call sheets. I thought I was being paranoid until Miranda began checking my expenses with the intensity of a vulture picking over bones. Then I sussed out something was definitely wrong. When she gave me a written warning, the company's equivalent of a yellow card, I knew she was out to get me. Not only that, but it was for being late! No one ever gets a written warning at IDX for being late.

Giles struts back to the table, sniffling his nose. Miranda's head shoots around in his direction. He smiles back. His pupils have expanded.

"That's better," he says, clapping his hands together. "Food arrived yet? I could eat a horse. Once at the Oxo Tower it took nearly an hour for my starter to arrive. I'm a patient kinda guy, but that's just taking the piss. Do you know what I mean, fella?"

He doesn't give me the chance to answer.

"Ever had problems like that?" he says, looking at Miranda. "I bet they wouldn't dare to treat a beautiful lady like that, not in a million years. I'm normally really into the Oxo Tower, it's got wicked views, and the..."

I switch off, Giles is doing my head in. His visit to the toilet appears to have given him a sudden burst of energy. I strongly suspect this is down to chemical stimulation. Miranda obviously has similar beliefs as she is now held enrapt by Giles's babbling, probably hoping he will sort her out later, too.

I've never been as much into cocaine as my workmates. Not only is it a rip-off, but it also turns people into walking egos. They suddenly think they are the most interesting subjects in the world. Conversation becomes an entirely one-way process, a bit like watching a *BBC Two* documentary entitled *'Why I am so cool'*. The rest of the office doesn't share my view. Come Friday, at 5.31pm, the toilets sound like a Hoover testing lab. We even have our very own in-house dealer, 'Charlie' Peters. He's meant to work on admin, but most of his Excel spreadsheets concentrate on who owes him what. Every Monday morning he comes round taking orders. He's the most popular man in the building.

The starters arrive and, true to form, mine is so small it takes me only two mouthfuls to empty my large white plate. Giles hasn't stopped talking long enough to eat his. Miranda pushes her food around, seemingly gripped by Giles' latest topic of conversation – the injustices of the football First Division play-off system. I'm surprised to find that Giles is into football, he has rugby written all over him. Presumably it's just another element of his ad agency persona.

His noise is getting on my nerves. I wonder if he'll take another trip to the gents. The thought of him larging it up while wrecking my life gets my back right up. Necking the rest of my wine, I decide not to just sit back and let him get away with it. I pull out my mobile and study it. I wonder if I have the courage to follow through with what in normal circumstances would seem a ridiculous plan. This question is answered when, after spewing bollocks for a further twenty minutes, Giles announces that he doesn't know what's wrong with his bladder. I give him thirty seconds, take a deep breath, and follow him to the toilet.

"Where you going?" Miranda says.

"I need to go, too."

"I hope that's all you need."

I ignore her and make my way to the gents. The marble/black wood theme makes me feel like I've just walked back into the eighties. Only one cubicle is closed. I enter the one next door, stand on the toilet seat and poke my head over the partition. Giles is busy chopping up two thin white lines with his credit card. I duck back down and pull out my mobile. My hand shakes a little as I turn on the video function. I sneak my head back over and film Giles rolling up a twenty quid note and snorting the lines up his nose. When he's finished, he flicks his head like in a hair advert, only to freeze halfway when his eyes catch mine.

"What the fuck are you doing, fella?" he says, dusting the toilet seat in panic.

"Just watching you doing illegal class A drugs in work time."

He gives a nervous laugh. "Yeah, good one. Funny. Listen, fella, you won't tell anyone, will you? Do you fancy a line?" He starts fumbling in his pocket.

"I'm alright, thanks. Look, I've never been a grass, but sometimes it can be difficult to keep things like this to yourself. Particularly when the person asking you to help him is shafting you by putting all his client's money into another magazine."

Giles steams out of the cubicle and squares up to me.

"I hope you're not threatening me, fella."

"I'm just telling you how it is."

"Who you going to grass me up to? Do you really think my boss will take the word of a sales rep over that of one of his key media buyers?"

"No, I don't think so. Unless, of course, there was a small videoclip to back-up the sales rep's word."

"What's that supposed to mean?"

"Think mobile technology," I say and walk out. As I sit down, Miranda scrutinises my eyes. Giles returns to the table frowning. He glares at me and bangs his knife on the plate.

"Where the fuck is that ladyboy?" he says.

"Who are you talking about?" Miranda says.

"The idiot French queer we have as a waiter."

"What do we need him for? You've not even finished your starter yet," I say.

Giles gulps the rest of his Chateauneuf du Pape. "Maybe not, but I've finished my drink."

The meal goes downhill after that. Giles gets increasingly agitated and Miranda, arriving to the conclusion that Giles won't be offering her a pick-me-up, gets increasingly bored. He starts to grill her on the type of mobile phones her company gives to its sales people. She's very unresponsive, which makes him even more agitated. We don't bother with dessert, much to the relief our waiter, who's become the brunt of Giles' anger. When I pay, I leave him a large tip.

Miranda demands another cab despite the office being only about a five minute walk away. While she waits inside, I shake hands with Giles. His palm is sweaty and his grip is far too hard.

"I want an agreement for twenty-four exclusive pages in our magazine by the end of the day," I say.

"You've got nothing on me," he says, pumping my hand harder.

"I'll email you when I get back to the office so you can see what nothing looks like."

"You're bang out of order," he says and storms off.

I don't feel out of order, I feel on top of the world. Miranda, on the other hand, looks as if she's just spent lunchtime watching paint dry. She doesn't say anything until the cab drops us off at the office.

"That was a complete waste of time," she says. "I think losing such a big account could well be the final nail in your coffin, particularly as the managing director has just asked me to cut costs in our division. In fact, I think I'll go and talk to him about you this very minute."

"What is your problem with me?"

"I can't stand arrogance," she hisses. "You think far too much of yourself. There aren't many people who get the opportunity I offered you."

"It was nothing personal. I had a girlfriend."

"Don't you dare patronise me," she says and steps into the lift.

I will never understand women. They have a unique way of thinking. I sometimes wonder if they experience a different reality. When Sadie phoned to say she'd been having a fling, she tried to blame me.

"What the fuck do you mean it's my fault?" I shouted.

"I know you've been playing around," she said.

"Playing around? What planet are you on?"

"I can tell. It's the way you act, the way you take so much time choosing what to wear in the morning. The way you spend hours trimming your beard."

"That's for work!"

"The way you're always late."

"That's the trains."

"And drunk."

"I've got to go out with my clients."

"And spend far too much time with Miranda." She says her name like an insult.

"She's my boss, for God's sake."

"Sorry, but you drove me to it."

I slammed the phoned down. I couldn't handle her voice anymore. I thought about going to the school and beating the shit out of the PE teacher, but then realised I'd probably get a pasting. I've never been any good at fighting, and a male PE teacher, by virtue of his profession, was likely to be considerably harder than me. I only saw Sadie once more, when she came round to collect the stuff she'd accumulated at my place. While my feelings yo-yoed between anger and lust, she never once lost her aura of self-righteous indignation. Even the memory pisses me off, so I stop thinking about it and return to my desk.

"How did it go? Did you dazzle Miranda with your sales genius?" Skinner says.

"Let's just say I'm quietly confident they will once again grace the pages of *Smart Car World*," I say, writing my email to Giles.

"That's strange. I got the impression from Miranda that the whole day was a right royal fuck-up."

"For all of Miranda's many talents, I'm not sure she always has a firm grip on the intricacies of the sales process." I start to download the videoclip of Giles onto my computer.

"Brilliant! You can be such a comedian sometimes. Miranda's never wrong, which is why she's a sales director and you're not."

"There's a first time for everything," I say, attaching the file to my email and clicking send.

I wonder how long it will take Giles to respond. He could still call my bluff, in which case I'd be screwed. Even though he gets on my nerves and I really don't want to be sacked, I'm not sure I could destroy someone's career over a bit of advertising.

I kill some time by going over to Gidders' desk. He's lounging in his chair, chewing a pen. He sits opposite the managing director's office. Through the glass wall, I can see Miranda, deep in conversation.

"Alright mate, how was your meeting?" Gidders says.

"Don't know yet. It could be that it went brilliantly, it could be that it went like shit."

"How can you not know? You were there, weren't you? Been going crazy on the wine again?"

"No, it's just that things are still a little bit up in the air."

"Well, fingers crossed. Miranda doesn't seem very confident, though." He nods in the direction of the office. "She's been in there with Ming ever since she got back."

Chris, our managing director, isn't Chinese but, like Flash Gordon's nemesis, he is merciless. He only ever seems to leave his office when he goes to the toilet, when he has lunch and when he destroys people. Maybe that's what managing directors are for, to act as caged threats, like sadistic jack-in-the-boxes. I've only ever had one job, if you discount paper delivering, dishwashing, apple-picking, burger-flipping, strawberry-packing, dartboard manufacturing and market researching, so I can't know for sure if he's a typical example of a company leader. If he is, then that might explain why the suited drones that trudge to my train station every morning look so grim.

Gidders' phone rings. He spins in his chair like Captain Kirk and grabs the receiver with a flourish. I leave him to it and stroll back to my desk. It's coming to the time in the afternoon when people are getting ready to go home. There's not the same buzz fizzling through the air as when everyone's charged on caffeine and optimism. We're always told that mornings are the prime selling time, which suggests to me that afternoons are not. When I sit down, Skinner leers at me.

"Giles Harcourt rang," he says.

"Why didn't you get me?"

"I didn't know where you were."

"What did he say?"

"He said to tell you to go fuck yourself."

"Yeah, very good, funny man. What did he really say?"

"Look, I even wrote it down." He holds up a post-it note. "He said he's sending you an email. Presumably to confirm all those ads that will once again grace the pages of *Smart Car World*," he says, mimicking my voice before cracking up with laughter.

I slump in my chair. I have a strange hollow sensation in my stomach, similar to how I felt when my cat was run over. I can't bear to look at Skinner, so I stare at my desk. It's a mess, a collage of papers, magazines, empty plastic cups, newspapers and pens. It's a unique arrangement, the flotsam and jetsam of my working day washed up by countless little waves of activity. I've never been the most organised person, but now I find myself eager for some order in my space. I grab a pile of stuff and push it into my drawer. The sight of the wooden surface makes me feel a bit better, so I clear away some more. Skinner has stopped laughing.

"Clearing your desk already?" he says.

My phone rings before I can answer him. It's Miranda.

"Can I see you in Chris' office? We'd like a word."

Before I get up, I see that Giles' message has arrived. I'm about to have a look when Miranda sticks her head out of the door and bawls at me to hurry. The whole office stops what they're doing. Every head turns in my direction. I feel as if I'm walking the plank in front of a football crowd. It's a relief when she closes the glass door.

"Afternoon Duncan, take a seat," Ming says without looking up.

I slide into the chair.

"I hear you went to see Giles Harcourt today," he says, finally lifting his head.

"Yes," I say, unable to form a more complex sentence.

"I hear it didn't go very well."

"I wouldn't necessarily say that. Giles has agreed to look at a proposal for the luxury car supplement."

"And that's good enough, is it? They are a world-renowned brand. Do you know what it does to the reputation of the magazine when we fail to carry a single page of their advertising?"

"It doesn't make us look very good," I say.

"Too damn right it doesn't! Your sales director tells me we used to have a market share on them, before you took the account over."

"That's not fair. I've only had it for…"

"Life's not fair. She also tells me you have an attitude problem. We haven't got room for slackers in this company. Are you a slacker, Duncan?"

"No, I'm not. I work as hard as anyone here, including my

sales director."

I expect this final act of courage to be the end. I wonder who'll explode first.

"You've got no idea how hard I work," Miranda says.

"Go and get your call sheet," Ming says.

I'm so surprised by this reprieve that I have to fight an urge to thank him. I may be going down, but at least it'll be with a bit of dignity. While I'm rummaging round my desk, I read Giles' email.

"You're a fucking arsehole," it says. "However, having gone through the circulation figures and analysed the editorial, I've come to the conclusion that *Smart Car World* represents a better proposition for my client. As a consequence, I've decided to book twenty-four exclusive pages. I expect a premium position for my client."

My heart pumps faster as I click open the attachment. It's an order form worth £138,000. I bang the keys of my calculator as though crushing ants. The little numbers tell me I've just earned over £4,500 in commission. I punch the air.

"What's the matter with you?" Skinner says. "Are you having a fit or something?'

"No, I'm celebrating twenty-four exclusive pages." I raise both my arms aloft.

"Yeah right, course you are. Would that twenty-four pages be from the same bloke who less than fifteen minutes ago told you to fuck off?"

"The very same," I say as I print out the order form. "It appears he's been swayed by my sophisticated sales pitch."

Skinner snatches the form from me.

"Who's the daddy now?" I ask, snatching it back. He doesn't reply. He doesn't need to, as we both know the answer. I make my way back into Ming's office.

"Let's have a look, then" he says.

"I couldn't find it."

"This is exactly what I mean by attitude," Miranda says. "You ask him to do one simple thing and he screws it up."

"Would you call twenty-four exclusive pages a screw-up?"

"What?" she says. "You wouldn't know twenty-four pages if they came up and slapped you in the face."

"Miranda, please. This is not a playground," Ming says and takes the sheet of paper off me. His expression doesn't change as he reads it. "Well, I must say, I'm impressed. It seems your meeting wasn't quite the disaster I was led to believe. We've never had exclusive business from them before. This obviously makes the rest of our conversation redundant. If you wouldn't mind, I now need to have a word with your sales director, alone. I'll be announcing your success to the rest of the company tomorrow morning. Excellent work, Duncan. Keep it up."

I thank Ming and strut out, flashing Miranda a smile as I go. She looks away and starts fidgeting with her pen. Skinner's nowhere in sight when I get back to my desk, so I put my hands behind my head and wallow in the warm glow of success. They say fortune favours the brave and I congratulate myself on proving this proverb true. I think about my talents being broadcast to the entire sales team tomorrow, a sales team that's probably expecting to hear about my imminent departure. I can't stop smiling.

I try to remember the last time I was bigged up in public. It was more than half a lifetime ago, when I was eleven and had come third in the county cross-country championship. Mum and dad came to the assembly to watch as the school presented me with a special certificate. I was so proud. It was brilliant having everyone applauding my achievement. It suddenly dawns on me that there's no way tomorrow will be the same. Not because I haven't done something worthy of praise. In our company's world, twenty-four exclusive pages is the equivalent of an Olympic gold in cross-country. It's the manner of my victory. When I came third in that race, I'd run so hard I thought I'd die, but getting these pages was nothing to do with skill or hard work. This makes the happy glow evaporate. I feel like a fraud. I don't want to work in a place that turns me into a cheat.

I realise that today's been special. It's given me an opportunity to do something I've wanted to do for a very long time. It's salvaged my reputation and earned me a fat commission cheque but, more than that, it's offered me a chance to try a different type of life. I've got no excuses. If I don't do it now, I'll soon find reasons not to do it at all. I'll bottle it until I'm suffocated by my comfortable lifestyle. I pull my keyboard closer and start to type. Even writing the words makes me shudder with excitement. Every extra letter is inching open the door to a world of new possibilities. I feel like I'm writing a love letter to a girl I've lusted after for ages, but never had the courage to tell. However, the email address is Miranda's. In the title box I write 'Letter of resignation'. I hesitate for a second longer, enjoying the feeling of imminent freedom, then click send.

For some reason I expect something to happen immediately. A fanfare or an eruption of fireworks, but all I see is people getting their stuff together and drifting out of the office. I look at my watch; it's 5.34pm. The working day's been over for four minutes and I'm still here. I switch my computer off and grab my bag. If I run, I might still get the 6.12pm from Vauxhall, but I can't be bothered. Running for trains is something I used to do. Instead I decide to take my time and enjoy the walk, just like I did this morning.

Sunday

By
Sophie Mackintosh

Sunday

For a moment when I wake up, I see the sun streaming through my window and I feel a flash of happiness. I feel its warmth on my skin and luxuriate in its feeling, for one golden second. And then I remember what day it is, and immediately the golden second is tarnished. In another time I would have looked out of the window and marvelled at the sky, the azure expanse so smooth as to look painted, with peaks and flurries of whipped-cream clouds drifting lazily above my head. But not in this time.

Now I burrow my head into my pillow and try not to remember. Trying to forget about days like these where I used to walk with Sylvie to the park and push her on the swings, where we would fly kites and she would scream with happiness. Her tiny face, with her downy blonde hair, and the adorable little outfits that I would choose for her every morning…trying to forget these things is impossible. I feel that perhaps she was woven into my DNA the moment she was born. Your child is a piece of you, a part of you. A close entwined bond is always there, even if you are the only one mature enough to realise it initially. You will always feel the graze of a small knee, the sting of a wasp, the stub of a fragile toe. When older, I imagine you will also feel the uncertain happiness of a first boyfriend, the disappointment of a failed exam, the pain of a first-broken heart. I will never know these things; I shall never see Sylvie grow older.

There is only one way to stop me thinking like this, and that is to get up and do something. So I do – slowly, stiffly, I get up and go to the bathroom. In the mirror my face is swollen, eyes sore. There are furrows around my brow and deep crevices, like scars, around my mouth. Forty-five is too young to look old, surely? I can never decide whether Sylvie's death made me an old woman or whether I looked like this all along and was too contented to notice.

The Remarkable Everyday

I used to look young. When I got married I was a blithe twenty-something, with peachy skin and shiny eyes. The ritual of makeup was something Roger never understood, but for me and my friends it was always important, the basis of many a phone-call and teenage slumber party. After being a gawky teenager with pale skin and curly hair, which never curled just right, it was peculiar and liberating to realise that with the right makeup (and not just frosted lip gloss and nuclear eye shadows) I could look pretty. Attractive. Maybe beautiful.

My ritual was secretive and I never let Roger see when I was working my magic. In this same bathroom I would sit, surrounded by tiny bottles and tubs of potions, all with bewitching names such as 'Allure' and 'L'amore'. In the hush of the bathroom I would mix, and daub, and paint, concentrating fully on getting everything perfect. My feather-light hands would flutter like moths around my hair; they would not even tremble as I lined my eyes with precision. I would flutter my inky eyelashes at the mirror, surrounding eyes that were suddenly mysterious and sultry. Then I would saunter into our bedroom and watch Roger's own eyes widen with surprise.

I am shocked suddenly to find myself crying again. Of course, even this memory is connected to Sylvie. We used to play with my makeup. I would put sparkle on her eyelids and a beauty spot on her cheek; she would wear one of my little-used evening dresses. She was only six, so it would trail on the floor behind her like a train. I used to giggle and pretend she was a film star, and she used to strike a pose and insist I took a photo. I hardly ever wore makeup myself after she was born, only when we went out, which was less and less as the years wore by. I planned to teach her about it prop-erly when she was older. When she was a teenager, I would pass on my secrets; we would mix, and daub, and paint our faces together.

I place my hands on the porcelain sink to steady myself. Get a grip. How long will it be before these memories make me glad, make me remember the good times without stabbing me with grief? That is the only way I can describe it, that breathless, painful tremble in my side. It's similar to being winded from a kick in the stomach.

Today is Sunday, so at least I do not have to face my students. People think that I am glad for my job, that teaching a class of monosyllabic sixteen-year-olds about Shakespeare will stop me thinking and remembering for a while. And it does help, I suppose. It's just that every time I see my class I am reminded, once again, that Sylvie will never get this far. She was only in her first year of school. I used to wait for her with the other parents by the school gates, a mixture of relief and dread in the air. My heart would leap when I saw her fair head in the crowd of bolshy children, and she would slip her sticky, warm little hand in mine as we walked home.

I splash my face unenthusiastically with cold water in a half-hearted attempt to make it look more human. I brush my teeth and drag a comb through my unruly hair. Thank God it's not a weekday because I really can't face having to look half-decent right now. At home I can let myself go because no one sees me. In the week I put on a spot of lipstick and do my hair, and while everyone thinks 'Good, Rachel's finally getting back to normal, terribly sad, but you have to move on', I know the real reason. I hate pity; sympathy embarrasses me. It is better to make a bit of an effort and therefore avoid the curious glances and pep-talks from my ex-husband.

My ex-husband. How strange that sounds. I try saying it out loud – "Roger, my ex-husband". My tongue falters over the unfamiliar contours of the word. "Remember how happy we were when we were younger?" I tell my reflection. My face stares back impassively, but I remember. I feel slightly crazy. Why am I standing here, talking to my reflection, getting bogged down by nostalgia? I have spent an hour in the bathroom. I shake my head violently and walk out, back into my bedroom.

I think about staying in my pyjamas for the rest of the day. The thought is tempting, comforting, but in the end I open my cupboard and try to focus my mind on choosing an outfit. To be honest, I don't care what I wear anymore, but every thought, no matter how mundane or trivial, takes up a minute or two of my time. I am sure that time used to pass more quickly, although when Sylvie was alive I always had something to do. Even when she was at school, there was always a pile of washing to sort out, spaghetti hoops and chicken nuggets to buy, or a ketchup-splattered kitchen to clean. It used to amaze me, how one tiny person could fill my day with work; how just the everyday routine of Sylvie's life used to exhaust me. The washing used to take longest – I could never get used to the sheer smallness of her clothes, the dinky doll-sized socks, the Lilliputian t-shirts and leggings, the flounced skirts and party dresses, which no mother can resist. I could sit there for hours, just gazing fondly at the precious garments, inhaling Sylvie's scrumptious baby-like scent. Talcum powder and skin with overtones of sweets and soap. Clean and fresh, and slightly grubby, just like all small children. Now time is viscous and as sticky as treacle, flowing slowly, painfully along.

The most heart-breaking moment involved the washing. It happened a few days after her funeral. I had somehow got through the death and the days after it, running on autopilot. It felt as if Sylvie was just away for a while, perhaps visiting her grandmother, and soon she would be home again, running through the door and barrelling into me with all her prodigious energy. Soon she would be home, brimming with adventures and stuffed with her grandma's home baking, and so I carried on numbly, waiting for her to come back.

Everyone left my house, eventually. Roger and his new wife had been visiting every day and every room was full of grieving friends and relatives. The kitchen groaned under the weight of cakes and pies that I would never eat, and every table in the house was suffocated by bosky groves of sympathy cards. I drifted from room to room, unsure of what to do. The house was spotless, the washing all completed. I found myself in Sylvie's room, sitting gingerly on the end of her bed. That felt wrong, so I stood up and started to put everything away, all her mess cleared up methodically as I had done so many times in the past. This was the only room left uncleaned – the only room where the relatives and friends had not dared to enter. In just a few days, it had been transformed from a colourful boudoir filled with her noise and laughter to something unmentionable, sacred. Even the walls seemed paler, the raspberry pink less vibrant and bold. I folded up her beautiful clothes and put them in the right place in her wardrobe. I picked up the discarded books by the side of her bed and put them in the bookcase. I fetched the vacuum cleaner and let the noise fill the house. For a minute the sound, which had always seemed so grating and obtrusive, was comforting and familiar, the sound of my everyday domestic life. But when all the dust had gone and it was switched off, the house seemed even emptier.

I looked underneath the bed and found a crumpled t-shirt. Pale pink, delicate, ruffled at the neck and unbearably childish. I slowly stroked it, running my hands over the creased fabric, holding it gently to my face. A huge wave of sadness broke over me. How many times had I told her not to do that? How many times had I told her off for not putting her clothes into the laundry basket? How had I dared to tell my precious angel not to do anything? My voice seemed caught in my throat for a second and then exploded in a cry of anguish. I started crying, properly, for the first time since the accident. These were not proper, television-funeral tears, but rather that unphotogenic wailing that leaves your face raw, and your body frozen and exhausted. My fists thumped the ground as if I was having a tantrum, my eyes scrunched up like a new-born's. Tears scalded my face and soaked the t-shirt, which I pressed to my eyes. Sylvie's baby-like smell was still on the material, and I cried harder, my memory of her face and laugh floating in front of my eyes, as misty as smoke and as tangible as my own hand. I don't know how long I stayed in her room, but I know that the light had changed and by the time I crawled, still weeping, into my own bed, it was past midnight. As I lay there, bathed in moonlight, with the curtains still open, I knew she wasn't coming back. I crawled to the window and shut the curtains, then collapsed back into bed, crying weakly in the darkness.

On remembering this, the tears threaten to start again. I start vigorously folding my clothes, looking for a clean t-shirt, forcing myself to think of something ordinary. What should I do today? What can I do? My thoughts answer me with 'nothing'. It's Sunday, what is there to do? Not even any decent television. I suppose I could get a video.

The phone rings, startling me. I clear my throat and manage a hoarse "Hello?"'

"Rachel, it's Roger. How are you?"

"I'm fine," I lie glibly. I am not fine. I'm glad Roger phoned instead of coming round. It's much easier to lie over the phone, where words are not contradicted by gestures and expressions. Lately, I hate people asking how I am, even though deep down I know it's an innocent question. It's just – how do they think I am? How would they react if I replied with "I'm terrible, actually, my daughter is dead; I miss her like nothing else. I have a horrible wrenching feeling in my gut all day because I miss her so much. Sometimes it is so painful I go and curl up in her bed and cry; I pull her Barbie duvet up around my ears and stay there all day. Yourself?"

Roger's voice is guarded and slightly stiff. I know that Sylvie's death was difficult for him too. But she was only two when he left, and he saw her only on Saturdays. I was with her every day. I cooked for her, read her stories – the intricacies of my life intertwined with hers. My life centred on hers. He had quality time with Sylvie, time which he marked down in his diary and struggled to think of things to do. Sunday was a special day for Sylvie and I – it was our day and no one else's. It wasn't quality time; I never thought of it as time that I had to spend with my child in order for her to grow up happy, for her to have a clear picture of family life. The love I felt for my daughter was all-consuming, enchanting. I spent Sundays playing with Sylvie because I wanted to. Ideas for games flew forth from our minds effortlessly, fluidly. We laughed till our sides hurt, we read stories, dressed up. Sunday was the happiest day of the week, unspoiled by school and work.

I force myself to make chit-chat with Roger, racking my brain for things to say. Something hangs between us in the air, unspoken. Today is three months since Sylvie's death, and that fact is like a wall of ice between our voices. I can tell that he wants to talk about it, but I am nowhere near ready. Maybe one day we will be able to talk and laugh and reminisce about her cute little ways, about long summer days at the beach, about her ballet shows. Perhaps one day we will be able to talk about what could have been.

Roger starts to cry on the other end of the phone, and I don't know what to say. His voice is thick with tears; I hear his undignified sniffing. It's funny how revolting people sound when they cry. I tense up and listen detachedly as I hear Roger's wife murmur to him in the background. In the end, she takes the phone and tells me he'll phone back later. I say that's fine, coolly, and hang up.

I still haven't had breakfast, so I make my way downstairs, trailing my hand languidly along the banister. I don't feel hungry in the slightest, but I force myself to see what I have to eat. Eating hasn't really featured on my list of priorities recently. I have lost a lot of weight, actually reaching the weight I was when I first married Roger, but, surprisingly, I don't care. I miss my comforting roundness, the cuddliness that made me feel like a proper mummy. I never really lost my pregnancy weight, I suppose. Now there is no physical proof that I even had a daughter, except for the eight silver stretch marks on my stomach. I stand there in the kitchen for a moment and think; even my body knows that Sylvie is gone. The wobbly stomach that Sylvie liked to bounce on is almost flat. My plump cheeks that she kissed every day are gaunt. The mother she loved was soft and 'cushiony' to her, while to everyone else I was ugly and fat. Now, without her, I think that I'm shrinking.

What should I have: boiled egg, cereal? I have time to make whatever I want. I decide on boiled egg with toast soldiers, a little child's breakfast. I made it often for Sylvie. Now I think how comforting the golden yolk and crispy toast would taste with a cup of tea. I boil the water, drop in the egg, set the timer. I make my toast, butter it well, and serve it with a flourish on my favourite plate. It looks appetising, but when I come to eat it, I find I simply can't. The yolk is like phlegm, cloying and sickly. My toast is brittle and tastes like card-board. Disgusted, I tip the lot in the bin.

Then what? I sit stiffly on a chair in the kitchen. The winter sunshine is still shining, streaming through the windows, casting puddles of light on the rustic stone floor. I touch the edge of a puddle with a toe and feel the warmth of the sun for the second time today. Little flecks of dust float in these spills of light. I think how much they remind me of glitter, or of minuscule moths. They always seem alive. Outside it is crisp and bitingly fresh – sunny but cold. I venture to the window and open it, breathing the freezing air deep into my lungs. The grass is studded with ice, my flowers dead after this sudden cold spell. Still, they look strangely picturesque, frost curlicues and embellishments turning their blackened petals to lace. Almost without realising it, I pull on my coat and walk out of the front door.

Actually standing in my garden, the light is brighter than it looked from the window; it is colder as well. I love this cold, despite myself. I always think it's so refreshingly clean. Today the air has the unsullied purity of iced water and, despite the goose bumps on my body, I feel better than I have for a long while. My feet start walking of their own accord, the grass clinking with every step. Where to go? I'm not sure. I decide to walk into the middle of town. So I do, but with every step, a vague feeling starts nagging at my mind. I stand still and will the feeling to become stronger. I think to myself, 'what do I need?' And the answer comes back, simple and strong. I need to feel close to Sylvie.

Perhaps it is the thinking and crying that I have been doing this morning, or the effect of the morning air, but the tears do not come. It feels natural. I want to feel close to my daughter. I want to go to the places we used to visit, to imagine her hand in mine, not to grieve, but to remember our happiness.

This is what I will do. I think for a second about phoning Roger and asking him to come with me, but I discard the thought almost immediately. This is something I want to do by myself. I carry on walking towards the town, but now with more purpose in my step, and a strange knot in my stomach – a mixture of dread, aching happiness and yearning.

In town it is busier than usual for a Sunday, and I only realise why when I see Christmas decorations in the shop windows. Only a couple of weeks left now, and the shops have started opening seven days a week to maximise the selling potential. Difficult to believe I'd forgotten all about it. I put the thought of how difficult this Christmas will be firmly out of my mind and instead watch the multicoloured throng of people passing me by in a steady stream. Harassed mothers trying to juggle a handful of children and bags are the main element of the crowd, with a few pained-looking men and small clusters of sniggering teenage girls. I see one of the mothers look at me with what seems like envy. I try to imagine who she sees – a woman who can do the most fantastic things, like go shopping with no dribbling baby attached to her hip, who could wander around town all afternoon, who could sit in a café and drink hot chocolate and watch the crowds all day. She catches me looking at her and smiles guiltily. I don't tell her that I would give up an eternity of freedom just to have my Sylvie back. I would gladly spend every day Christmas shopping with a sulky little child, complete with tantrums, bribes and breakdowns, if only it meant I would have my daughter back. In my own way, I envy the mothers and I envy the teenage girls as well. Their lives at the moment are relatively unscathed, with only exams and boyfriends to worry about. I watch them shriek and giggle, hunched over glittery mobile phones, and their high heels and elaborate hairstyles make me think again of what Sylvie could have been.

As a teenager, I imagine Sylvie would have been beauti-ful. She would keep her billowing blonde hair and, by the time she was fourteen or so, it would reach her waist. She always had it long – I could never bear to cut it off. My own hair was usually cut short in some unflattering bob when I was small, but Sylvie's hair made her look like a fairy princess. Her huge green eyes would be lined with eyeliner and she would have fluttery mascara eyelashes. Her mouth would be shiny with strawberry lip gloss; she would still be quite small and thin...petite. I would take her shopping, just like a friend, and we would gossip over skinny lattes and blueberry muffins. She would try on tiny little clothes, and I would jokingly gasp with outrage but let her have them any-way, because I never could deny her anything. We would laugh as I tried on the most outrageous outfits in the shop, and then she would encourage me to buy some crazy shoes – leopard-print? Fluffy? She would always be kind and graceful, sparkly and fun. She would have little braids in her hair and glittery butterfly clips. She would be popular and would do incredibly well in school. I imagined her going to Cambridge, being the best student they had ever had; I pictured her on her graduation, radiant and ecstatic in her mortarboard and black gown.

She would get married to a dashingly handsome, rich man who was wonderfully kind, worshipped the ground she walked on, and was insistent that she never, ever cooked unless she really wanted to. He would shower her with gifts and affection; they would have two perfect children – one girl, one boy – and she would live her life full of happiness with a wonderful family and a fantastic career, surrounded by love and gorgeous things for all her life.

I feel a twinge of sadness, but I put it to one side. I force myself to smile and carry on walking. Then I see the shoes.

Bright pink leopard-print boots, ridiculously high spindly heels, diamante trim around the top. Despite myself, I want them. I want those mad, extrovert boots. I want to proudly teeter around in them and see people's eyebrows rise and to laugh inside myself all day.

I try them on in the shop and test them out. I can only take mincing little steps and I dissolve into giggles. I look like mutton dressed as lamb, but I honestly don't care. It's been so long since I've been shopping, I've forgotten how fun it is. I buy the shoes, I buy a hot little dress to go with the shoes, and I buy an outrageous necklace to complete the outfit. I will probably never wear them, but it is enough to imagine Sylvie's teenage voice exclaiming "Mum! They're so cool!" My gift to myself.

The park is nearby now, which is where I'm heading. It is small and quaint, like something out of a story. The duck-pond is frozen over, and a group of children are laughing as a confused mallard slides around on the glassy surface. Poor duck. The swings where I used to push Sylvie are still creaky and a bit rusty. I am surprised to find that nothing has changed, although it has only been three months since I was last here, and not a lifetime as it sometimes feels. But it was another life, I think suddenly. My life before Sylvie died. I am irrefutably not the same person, at least not now, but maybe in a while I will be again? Or have I changed forever?

I go to the swings and sit on one. I don't care how stupid I look. This was Sylvie's favourite swing, candy-striped in red and blue. For a second I think I hear her gurgling scream of laughter, bubbling through the air like a brook. Her feet swinging up, higher, higher, as mine do now. The chains groaning as usual, and my familiar worry – will the swing break? The air swishes past me, making my eyes water from the cold. I swing and swing and swing, until the aching in my arms is unbearable and I have to get off.

Sunday

How many times have I been here? Too many to count. In summer, with scoops of strawberry ice-cream, pink tributaries running down the cone, baking sunshine above our heads. In spring, with ducklings in the pond, an irresistible lure to all the little girls in the area. In autumn, when the surrounding trees shed their rustling treasures, with Sylvie kicking her way excitedly through a pile of leaves. And in winter, on many days like this, wrapping Sylvie in a duffel coat and drinking hot chocolate at home afterwards. The pockets of my coat were always full of Sylvie's findings – an interesting pebble, a shell, a pretty leaf, and once a bird's egg-shell, blue-tinged and with a certain tensile beauty. Sylvie proudly kept it in a box in her room.

I am restless now, wanting to go somewhere else. But where? I gaze at my palms, streaked with red from the rusty chains of the swing, and I try to think. A sound decides it for me. In the air I can here the gentle chiming of a church bell. The thought of sitting there, breathing in the incense-scented air and letting the ancient words of the service flow around me is incredibly tempting. My world may be in disarray, the whole world in general may be changing, but the timeless quiet of the church will always go on, familiar and unaltered.

The church is quite near to the park, and I am caught up in the steady stream of people walking through its solid doors. This crowd is so much different to the one earlier, the hot and frazzled people in town. An air of steadiness and peace radiates from them; I feel calmer already. In the church they have started putting up decorations. Holly is strewn all around and an imperious Christmas tree stands next to the organ. It reminds me of Christmases past, of singing *'Silent Night'* with pink cheeks and a scarf wound round my neck. It reminds me of carol-singing nights with mince pies and steaming hot chocolate, and most of all it reminds me of my first Christmas with Roger.

We had an open fire and a small Christmas tree that we had spent most of the day decorating. Christmas was still fairly low-key – we were going to spend the day itself with my parents, saving us a lot of cooking and work. We had time then to relax in front of the television, watching festive rubbish and laughing together. We gorged ourselves on satsumas and leftover chocolate tree decorations. Acting like kids then was still adorable rather than immature, with no children of our own to lend us gravity or to demand our attention.

Later on we walked our way to church for the midnight service. Like today, the air was clean and freezing, reaching deep into our lungs. There was a light smattering of snow falling through the air. By the time we got there, our hair was festooned with speckles of white. The church was packed and the stained glass windows steamed up with a hundred people's foggy breath. My favourite part of that service, the part I remember the most vividly, was when we were each holding a candle and the lights were turned off. The flickering, delicate light swooped around the high ceiling of the church and shadows spilled from the corners. It suddenly seemed magical. I had never really been one for religion, but at that moment I felt closer to it than I ever did again in my life. The candlelight connected us all with its dainty threads of white gold, and I felt disappointed, sad almost, when the lights were switched back on.

Today there is no candlelight, but the sun shines through the stained-glass causing patches of red to glimmer on the floor, fading when the sun goes behind a cloud. The church is not quite as packed, but most of the pews are full. Other people are with families, but I sit here alone with only my memories. As well as a church where I have celebrated Christmas, weddings and christenings, this is also the church where Sylvie's funeral took place. I am sitting quite close to the front, and the vicar recognises me. At first he cannot quite place me – did I attend the last wedding? Has my child recently been christened? Then he realises and his smile is sympathetic, but slightly awkward, as he remembers the occasion when we last met.

It is difficult to stop the tears from welling up in my eyes, but I use every ounce of my concentration to stop them from running down my cheeks. I stare at the floor. The grey flagstones have been worn down, looking as soft as velvet due to the thousand different footsteps that have walked up and down this aisle.

Sylvie's funeral was in early September, when the sunshine was still dusky and warm with summer, and the leaves were still green. Like today, the stained-glass windows shone coloured light onto those same flagstones. Like at Christmas, the church was full to the brim with people, but they were dressed in black and crying over the death of a child, instead of rejoicing over a birth. Roger and I sat in the front pew. His second wife was next to him, and they cried together. I sat there, tears running down my face, but cold and angry at the same time. I remember thinking: 'She has no right to be here. Sylvie is nothing to do with her.' She was crying, the woman who saw her maybe once a week if she wasn't doing something more important.

I remember that there were pink roses decorating the church, and not holly. I chose the roses. In my eyes, Sylvie was too young for lilies, with their sickening funeral smell and waxy, unapproachable petals. Roses were sweet and pure and inoffensive so, yes, Sylvie would have roses. Although against the black of everyone's clothes, the blooms looked blowsy and inappropriate.

The coffin was small and white, with yet more roses heaped on top. I couldn't look as it passed us, carried on the shoulders of four solemn men. I kept looking straight ahead. There was organ music playing something suitably gloomy, and I suddenly felt like laughing. It reminded me of a wedding, with music playing as the radiant bride tripped down the aisle. But instead of laughing, more tears spurted out from my eyes.

The sun carried on shining, touching the roses with gold. The atmosphere was sad, yes, but gentle. Even though I thought the flowers looked slightly wrong in the end, their scent filled the church and it was soothing. My mother was sitting next to me, and I felt her shaking hand slipping into mine, just like when I was younger and needed consoling. With my other hand I traced the fragile engravings on the back of the pew in front of me. I concentrated on the swirls of dust caught in the dark wood and marvelled at the time and effort it must have taken to carve it. Roger stood up to give a reading, and I concentrated even harder, although my fingers slipped on the wood with nervous sweat. I could never have stood up there and given a reading. How could I have summed up Sylvie's short life in a few paragraphs? Roger's voice cracked as he spoke of her kindness and fun, and her popularity among her classmates. There was so much left unsaid. She wasn't always an angel, by any means. She could be naughty, and mischievous, but it was those times that made her human. Roger didn't mention any specific days in her life, any particular times, but my mind raced through the fun we had experienced, through the hugs and kisses and tickles, and I missed her with an excruciating ache.

We followed the pallbearers outside, into the small intimate graveyard. As they lowered the coffin into the grave, the volume of crying amplified. I kept concentrating on other things, trying to distract myself. My mouth was dry and tasted of cardboard, my tongue felt gritty. I concentrated on the sound of birdsong rather than think about Sylvie. My feet were uncomfortable in my new black shoes and I focused on the pain in my little toe rather than look at the coffin. I stared at the ground and watched a fat, shining beetle scuttle across the grass. When I heard the dry scatter of earth on wood, I knew it was almost over. As we left the graveyard, the grave was still being filled. I didn't look back once.

At my mother's house, the atmosphere was slightly more relaxed. The food and endless cups of tea were a welcome distraction, but I wasn't hungry at all. At my mother's insistence, I nibbled vaguely at a sausage roll, sipped at a cup of tea, but neither tasted of anything. So many people came up to me, wishing me well, crying on my shoulder. I was like a machine, perfunctorily patting them on their hand, soothing them in a monotone, when really I was the one who needed comforting. The sympathy was stifling and the room was humid. I had not eaten properly for days, so it's no wonder I started feeling sick.

I sat in the bathroom for a while, feeling clammy and sticky, and decidedly nauseated. Beads of sweat sat on my forehead, my hands twisted around each other, fidgety and knotted. I could hear the noise of people from downstairs and I wished that I was at home, curled up under my duvet, sleeping. I had not even had a decent night's sleep since the accident, my mind as restless as my hands. When I closed my eyes, I saw Sylvie's face. I saw her little figure running across the road, I saw the car…

Now, sitting in the church today, the memories are unflinchingly vivid. I suppose it's no wonder because three months is not a long time. I can only hope that time will dull them enough for me not to remember the expression of the driver and the exact tone of Sylvie's scream.

The service starts, and I relax. The vicar's words swirl around me. Like at the funeral, I trace the engravings of the pew. I look up at the walls and read the memorials. Some are simple, grey stone, like the floor, while others are carved in marble. I hate one of them – black, shiny marble with gold letters. It must have been expensive, but it looks cheap, too polished and hard.

Sylvie's gravestone was a teddy bear, painted and lovingly carved from stone. It stood out among the other gravestones, angels and crosses that were planted in the ground. There was no long inscription, just Sylvie's name and the necessary dates, and underneath was written 'I love you'. I didn't care at all if people thought it was clichéd or too sentimental. 'I love you' was the phrase that Sylvie said most often. She would tell me first thing in the morning, when she came home from school, and at night when I tucked her into bed. The day after the funeral, I placed a heap of yet more roses on her grave. That was the only time I could face going back there. At that point I was still somewhat anaesthetised by the shock and pain. The teddy bear sat there, plump and smiling, a bundle of flowers in its lap. I hoped that Sylvie could somehow look from wherever she was and notice that she had the happiest grave in the churchyard.

I stand up with the others in the church and I sing the hymn as loudly as I can. I always loved to sing, especially in church. I love the feeling of unity as a building full of strangers sing together, voices intertwining around the old, familiar words. I hear quivery old lady sopranos and booming bass voices, and above all the voice of the vicar leading the way. The sound is clear and powerful, each word ringing with meaning.

It's not long before the service ends. I look at my watch

and realise, to my surprise, that an hour-and-a-half has passed and it's now five in the afternoon. Laughter and chatting has replaced the quiet, expectant atmosphere, and people are starting to leave. I feel dazed that so much time has passed without me noticing. I stand up slowly and move towards the door, silent in the chattering crowd. The sun has faded outside, twilight rapidly darkening the golden hue, cooling the air further. I pull my coat around me, shivering, and start to make my way home – but I stop. I would like to visit Sylvie's grave, so I do.

Even though the weather lately has been blustery and wet for the most part, the teddy bear still looks perfect. Perhaps in a few years the paint will blister and erode from constant battering, but at the moment there is not a scratch on it. I crouch down and pat its head. In the darkness it looks like a real teddy bear, stuffed with sawdust and silky-furred. My roses must have long rotted away, but there is a fresh bunch of flowers there. It's almost too dark to read, but I can make out the words in the light of a nearby street lamp – 'To Sylvie, with all my love, your daddy'. In a strange way, this hurts. He has been able to visit here, to cry over her grave and to leave flowers. I always felt that I was the one who cared most, yet I had only been here once. I realise that I have been too upset and lethargic to come anywhere near here recently, but I still feel as though I have abandoned my daughter.

Abandoned her? I can't believe I am even thinking such a thought. After all the nights spent crying, after so many weeks lying in bed and being unable to move due to grief. Weeks of not eating and dragging myself to the school, thinking of her every minute of the day. I promise myself that now I seem to be feeling a bit better, I will come here more often. I will bring flowers each time.

It is now properly dark, and I walk out of the churchyard.

It will take me about twenty minutes to get home and I walk briskly to warm myself up. The air, which was so refreshing earlier, is now bitter. I am tired and just want to get home. For the first time in ages I find myself wishing for a cup of tea and some toast with jam. I reach the road near Sylvie's old school and rub my goose-pimpled arms as I wait for a break in the traffic. Then I realise where I am. I step back from the curb and start shaking. Across the road, on the opposite pavement, is a pile of flowers, slippery and rotten after three months of rain. Brown slimy petals are scattered on the tarmac.

Three months ago today I stood here with Sylvie. We had spent a quiet Sunday having lunch at my mother's house, and then I took Sylvie to the park. It was quite grey and overcast; the sky was heavy and the air was still warm. She was due to start year two the next day, and I wanted her last day of the summer holidays to be fairly low-key, so that she wouldn't be tired. Sylvie swung herself dizzy and played enthusiastically for half-an-hour, until it started to threaten rain. I could hear a faint grumble of thunder in the air and thought it would be better to get home quickly.

It started raining properly as we half-jogged back through town. Sylvie enjoyed the rain, splashing and spraying puddles gleefully until I almost lost my temper. I gripped her hand tight and told her to hurry up; we hadn't brought her coat and I was worried she would get drenched. This seemed like a very real possibility as the rain gradually became heavier, and Sylvie's hair was soaking around her shoulders by the time we reached the road.

It was difficult to see in the rain, which by now was almost a steady deluge of water. My hair was plastered to my head and my eyes were scrunched up as though I was swimming. The only way that I could see the cars was by looking out for the headlights. I stepped back from the curb, cursing, as a car drove past quickly and sprayed me from head to toe with yet more water. Sylvie giggled and I snapped at her. I hadn't meant to, but I was so worn out and soaked to the bone. Sylvie pouted and started to sulk. I sighed to myself and carried on watching the road. I let go of Sylvie's hand for a moment, to wipe the water from my eyes, and she was gone, her short legs running across the road. I stared after her, aghast, and screamed at her to come back. My eyes were wide with terror, my heart thumping in my chest. I thought she might make it to the other side, but a car driving quickly failed to notice her. Sylvie was caught on the bonnet and thrown into the air. She lay on the ground, limp and unmoving. Without thinking, I ran to where she lay, nearly getting knocked over myself, but my taller frame meaning that the cars saw me. By this time most of them were stopping anyway, realising that an accident had happened. I was beside myself.

"Call an ambulance!" I screamed, cradling Sylvie in my arms. A thousand different snippets of information that I had garnered from medical programmes and rudimentary first-aid classes started clamouring in my head. I realised that I shouldn't have touched Sylvie and, dreading that I might have hurt her further, I lay her tenderly on the ground. There was hardly a mark on her, except for a lump on her head that must have been from where she hit the road. Her eyes were shut tight. Rain and tears dripped from my face onto hers. I was crying and shouting incoherently, refusing to let go of her hand, even when the ambulance men arrived. In the ambulance I still clasped her hand assiduously, letting go eventually when the paramedics persuaded me to because otherwise they couldn't get to her to administer CPR.

The ambulance was a flurry of electric paddles and lowered voices by the time we reached the hospital. Sylvie's face was hidden behind a threatening-looking oxygen mask, her face drained and wan. She was wheeled into surgery straight away. How I wish we could have been waiting in accident and emergency, with the hassled nurses and other people with minor injuries. Sylvie being wheeled in this fast meant that something was seriously wrong. I clenched my fists tight, digging my nails into the palms of my hands to stop me from crying.

I sat in the waiting room for hours. All around me, obscenely colourful posters attempted to brighten the off-white walls. I looked at the poster showing cancer statistics against a magenta backdrop, glanced over the lime green and bright yellow poster warning against sunburn, tried to interest myself in an orange poster all about liver infections. It was no good. I picked up some magazines and tried to flick through them, but the words swam before my eyes. I went to the public phone and phoned my mother and Roger. I told them that Sylvie had been in a serious accident and they needed to come to the hospital now. Then I sat back down and waited.

Roger and my mother had arrived by the time the doctor came out to see me. The medic's face told me everything I needed to know – collapsed, defeated, weary-eyed. I curled up into a little ball on my chair and howled, while my ex-husband and mother sat there, numb with shock.

This time the weather is fine, although it's past six in the evening. I walk across the road and walk straight home. This day has been a step forward, certainly, but it has also been nerve-wracking. I feel wrung out, every ounce of energy and resistance squeezed out of me. I forget about the tea and I walk upstairs and start running a bath instead. The hot water fills the room with steam, billowing and writhing like smoke. When I look into the mirror, the steam curls around my head, and I stay watching myself until the mirror mists up completely. I turn off the bath taps and go into my bedroom.

Sunday

Methodically, leisurely, I choose my nightclothes and lay them on my bed. I decide against the bath. All I want to do right now is sleep, my head as foggy as the bathroom mirror.

I lie in bed, feeling exhausted and pale, sad but kind of happy at the same time, no matter how trite that sounds. I think I might be getting better. I don't pretend that it will happen at once – but today has been quite an experience. I feel closer to Sylvie. My hand strokes the cool expanse of my cotton bed cover, smoothing out creases and making me more comfortable. I plump up my pillow and spread myself out in a starfish shape. I can't believe that even though Roger has gone, I still sleep hunched up on my side of the bed. Stretched out like this, I feel deliciously relaxed and sleepy. As I start to drift off, I think to myself that today I have started to live again. It may only be small things that I have done, but now that I have done them I feel so much better. A small smile fleets across my face, a face that for once is not scalded with tears or crumpled in grief. And for the first time in three months, I fall asleep without having to cry to get there.